A Slant of Light

A Slant of Light

Contemporary Women Writers
of the Hudson Valley

Laurence Carr & Jan Zlotnik Schmidt
Editors

CODHILL

Codhill Press books
are published for David Appelbaum

First Edition
Printed in the United States of America

ISBN 978-1-930337-73-2

Cover and text design by Alicia Fox
Cover art by Amy Cheng, *Dusk Revisited,* oil on paper, 2010

Library of Congress Cataloging-in-Publication Data
A Slant of Light : Contemporary Women Writers of the Hudson Valley /
Laurence Carr & Jan Zlotnik Schmidt,
editors. — First edition.
    p.   cm.
Includes bibliographical references and index.
ISBN 978-1-930337-73-2 (alk. paper)
1. American literature—Hudson River Valley (N.Y. and N.J.) 2. American
literature—Women authors. 3. Hudson River Valley (N.Y. and N.J.)—Literary
collections. I. Carr, Laurence, editor of compilation. II. Schmidt, Jan Zlotnik,
editor of compilation.
PS548.N7S58 2013
810.8'0928709747--dc23
                                        2013019688

CONTENTS

❄ Gender and the Body

❋ Relationships

❊ Self in the World

INTRODUCTIONS

Laurence Carr & Jan Zlotnik Schmidt

For several years, I've wanted to create a third anthology for Codhill Press, to be a companion book to the previous published volumes, *Riverine: An Anthology of Hudson Valley Writers* and *WaterWrites: A Hudson River Anthology*. For both of these volumes, I read hundreds of pieces of writing (fiction, memoirs, essays, and poems) by hundreds of regional writers. And in each case, I was struck by the depth and honesty of the women authors who offered up their work.

Early on, the thought of creating an anthology that brought together some of the most interesting and imaginative writing by women authors of the Hudson Valley struck we as a worthy project, but I realized that I could not make this journey alone. I would need someone to accompany me who knew the territory as a writer and editor and who also brought a perspective about the issues on which the anthology could focus.

I contacted my friend and colleague, Jan Zlotnik Schmidt, Distinguished Teaching Professor at SUNY New Paltz, and an accomplished writer and editor of prose and poetry. I prepared my speech to try to coerce her into the project. I think I was at the end of my first sentence when she said, "Yes, I'd like to be part of this; the time is right for this book." Without need for further coaxing, we immediately got down to the "nuts and bolts": themes, structure, and a vision that would speak to contemporary readers. In a few moments, the book had leapt into existence.

As the months passed and word spread about the volume, the submissions started to pile up. Soon, Jan and I were looking at xii A Slant of Light

over 500 pieces of writing from over 150 Hudson Valley writers. We knew we couldn't include every piece, but tried to find those works that spoke to the five thematic sections that created the book's narrative: Mythos, Identity, Gender and the Body, Relationships, and Self in the World.

The title of the book emerged after months of reading: *A Slant of Light,* a nod to a poem by Emily Dickinson, our neighbor to the East.

Through research, I discovered how this volume builds upon the foundations laid by earlier writers who called the Hudson Valley home. The valley was fertile literary ground for many authors of prose and poetry from its early years, including: Susan Warner (*The Wide, Wide World* 1849, published under the pseudonym Elizabeth Wetherell. It is often acclaimed as America's first bestseller.); Anna Warner (who sometimes wrote under the pseudonym Amy Lothrop. She wrote thirty-one novels on her own, the most popular of which was *Dollars and Cents,* 1852); Mary Isabella Forsythe (*The Beginnings of New York, Old Kingston, The First State Capitol,* 1909); the poet Mildred Whitney Stillman (*Wood Notes,* 1922; *Pioneers,* 1926; and *Queens and Crickets,* 1927); and Anya Seton (*Dragonwyck,* 1945).

We hope that *A Slant of Light* will add to the rich legacy of works written by Hudson Valley authors and that it will both entertain and bring insight to everyone who reads these pages.

—*Laurence Carr*

At 7 a.m. when I walk my dog on my country road, the
Shawangunks almost pink in early morning light, I reflect,
allowing myself to let go of those gnawing anxieties or "to do"
lists that cloud the brain and drown out creative thought. In this
space of quiet, one morning I was thinking about the volume
Larry and I were editing, marveling at the richness and diversity
of the works and the range of women's voices. Indeed, the
Hudson Valley is a nourishing place, it seems, for women writers
to live and work.

I thought back to my own early days as a graduate student and
poet in the 1970s—the dearth of women's voices in the American
literature anthology that I taught from, the lack of women's
literature courses, and the few dissertations that there were on
my three chosen women writers, Edith Wharton, Ellen Glasgow,
and Willa Cather. I remembered the passion and political verve of
those second wave feminist scholars, determined to make visible
the invisible lives of women and create a more expansive literary
canon. These scholars wrote about the silences and anger of
women, phallocentric discourse, and the power of the patriarchy
to suppress women's voices and creativity. I thought of the many
conversations I had with my peers, women who were struggling
to unleash their voices, to feel entitled to write as women, to
write about different experiences and create in different ways
from men. During that time, several graduate students and I
organized a colloquium on contemporary women poets, focusing
on the work of Denise Levertov, Sylvia Plath, Anne Sexton, and
Adrienne Rich. The response from several of our male professors
shocked us: "Why would you study these women? There are no
women poets worth writing about. They are all minor figures."
We proceeded with the symposium; the room was packed.

That was 1973. In the past forty years, there has been an
outpouring of both scholarship about women's work, the
discovery of voices lost to history, and women's writing.

Certainly a more expansive and diverse literary canon has
emerged. This volume is part of that expanding literary tradition.
Adrienne Rich, who died this past year, would be pleased.
In an early essay, "When We Dead Awaken: Writing as Re-
Vision," she contends that "re-vision—the act of looking back,
of seeing with fresh eyes, of entering an old text from a new
critical direction—is for women more than a chapter in cultural
history: it is an act of survival." This process of re-envisioning
applies not only to critiquing literary texts, but also to reading
the texts of our lives: looking back on experiences from new
perspectives, exploring new paths for our futures. This process
of "re-vision" characterizes this volume. It contains re-imaginings
of myths for women, explorations of identity, body and gender
and relationships, and meditations on women's place in the larger
global world. We hope this volume adds to the conversations
about the experiences of women, reflecting life in the Hudson
Valley and beyond.

—*Jan Zlotnik Schmidt*

PART 1

MYTHOS

Wind Innuendo

Margo Taft Stever

So small
she cannot talk,
the child sits
in a field of
daffodils.
Her face
held close
to the blossoms
turns
slightly yellow
in sunlight.

Pollen grinds into
her hands.
Stems tickle her
backbone, thread
into her skin.

The thick
strings of stamen
lick her tongue.
Her petals bend,
always in wind.
To insects that enter,

each movement is
innuendo.
Her body opens
and opens, swills
in the billowing
spring light. ✽

reviving Coyote   *Claire Hero*

Coyote slinks out of the road & into my hands. Out of my hands
& into my mouth. With my teeth she bites the bark in two that
binds her. With my tongue she licks the placenta off the words.
Coyote steals out of my mouth & into my hair. Out of my hair &
into my skin. In my skin she drags the forest floor, looking for
the bodies. In my skin she hacks back the dark. (& who are those
masked that ring round the wood? —) Coyote sneaks out of my
skin & into my lungs. Into my nose. With my nose the earth is
clean as paper. Coyote scrawls herself across it, crawls into my
hands. With my hands she rends the voles in two. With my hands
she opens a door. Inside I am waiting. Inside I offer her a kind of
apple, some Indian cake, a bed of hides, & didn't we bed down,
Coyote & I, in this shabby cave while the hunters searched for
us in the vast boscage of the body? Didn't we couple in our fear?
Coyote runs over my snowy terrain, marking my skin with her
claws. How do I tell you that my body is the road upon which
Coyote dies? How do I rear what births from my mouth? ❀

Islanded

Jo Pitkin

Dark is *your* luxury.
Whenever at night
A wild iris scent
Snags above tides,
You take a night stroll.
Your path inclines
Toward ash-grey waves
Where gender dissolves
Underneath the black.
For me, every mango tree
With female fruit
Hangs heavily.
Refrain, refrain cracks
My palmetto-caned
Chair like dry husks
On coconut.
From my high porch roost,
I see star flame
Fling maps of light
On the open water.
Waves scatter them.
Men cannot catch them,
Those seven nymphs,
Who, for protection,
Were changed into doves
And doves into shy stars,
The strewn Pleiades.

Landlocked listener,
Must I be content
To decipher cries
That may be the cries
Petrels make at sea? ✺

Helen

Sylvia Barnard

Sappho told us long ago
how love is powerful
beyond all gods,
how Helen left
both child and parents
and a royal husband
to follow love to Troy.

I am a lover of men
as Helen was
but Sappho lover of women
speaks for all.

It is Eros, not Poseidon,
who shakes the earth
and batters the waves
of the sea.

It is Aphrodite
who makes our
menopausal breasts
grow hot
and brings weeping
to the middle-aged.

Imagine Helen
grasping the hand of Paris
and bidding him good-bye.

Still in Sparta
she tries to reconstruct
his voice and features
as he sails the Aegean
towards an unknown city.

Oh, imagine Helen
having let him go. ❈

Penelope

Joan I. Siegel

Who can say
she didn't put down that shroud
more than once
and step into

some lacy wine-dark thing
or a bit of flounce
in tangerine or cool lime

to show off
blackness of hair
skin sunbathed in Aegean waters
some fluff about the shoulders

collarbones and throat
just enough décolleté
and clinging? ❈

Hypatia   *Barbara Louise Unger*

Of the four women in *A Young Person's Guide*
to Philosophy, she has the only full-page
spread. Simone de Beauvoir has to share
hers with Sartre, and Luce Irigaray gets
a paragraph in back, along with
Mary Wollstonecraft, that *hyena*
in petticoats, that *philosophizing serpent*.

A gifted astronomer in Alexandria
when its lighthouse was one of the Seven
Wonders of the World, she was famous for
wisdom and beauty. She wore the white cloak
of a philosopher and drove her own chariot,
teaching *the One* to male aristocrats, and
to seek *the eye buried within*. When one
fell in love with her, she dangled her bloody
rags in his face and said, *This is what you*
love, young man, and it isn't beautiful.

When Bishop Cyril banished the Jews,
destroying temples and pagan statues,
her friend Orestes, the Roman governor,
protested. Cyril preached her black magic
had caused all the city's woes, till a mob
dragged her from her chariot, stripped her,
hauled her to the Caesareum, their new
church, flayed her with oystershells, scattered
her parts in the streets and burned the rest.

Hers was the first witch-hunt, also possibly
the plane astrolabe, brass hydrometer
and the hydroscope. Her work, too, was burned
with the great library. Cyril became a saint. ✸

Andromeda at Midlife   *Ann Cefola*

Why do I read my daily horoscope,
the sun's angle cast over lines, planets telling me
to avoid purchases or commitments?
I want to believe in this cosmic dance,
that slow-radiating waves pull at me like tides,
arrange a telephone call from someone I haven't heard from
in six years. Looking at the constellations, or the ring around
Saturn,
I need to believe in a pattern, a higher order, a face with designs
upon me, like the alarm that wakes me each day, reporter
breathless
with 6:30 a.m. crises. The idea that light so far away
    could ever reach or influence me.
I could study tea leaves, but I like the bigness up there,
the regularity of Orion arriving each winter, the exhaustion
    of Perseus running.
I think there is room for me, too, a constellation, a myth,
    a woman of 43
constantly looking up and wondering, who realizes at last
the dipper is full, the hunter will never catch the bear and
Andromeda must unloose her own chains, rub her rusty wrists,
stretch, then sit down and cast her future in stars. ❉

An Explanation to My Husband
for Christa McAuliffe

Lisa Fleck Dondiego

I knew I wanted to go, defying tugs of gravity,
children, love, when I saw that shot

of earth, the blue and solid one, sailing
in a cloudless sky. I had to see

that earth, ride high,
try to reach that spot in space.

I needed to make space
real, bring it home to the children,

eyes turned up in awe,
seeing through my eyes.

That freezing day we went nose-up,
full-throttle in fire-streamed flight

I held my breath at first, hoping to breathe
at last the freedom space can give.

But then, hopes contracted, shrunk
to nothing, sputtering to silence.

And you, the rooted one, fixed foot
of my compass—so distant

you could no longer see my eyes,
or feel my electronic, blue pulse

growing fainter and fainter
until space was all I knew —

what could I, so far away
and blown apart, impart?

The surest challenger is death?
No. For a while, at least, I flew. ❋

Madonna Bomb   *Celia Bland*

There are no words to describe the way she hunches
belly resting on thigh, key turned on and she cannot
turn it off, working the brake with her other foot. It's hard to see
into the distance, sitting like that.

She drives a dichotomous street,
the blood flowing in and out, birth and death, every turn
leading to this one and a line of Hummers, the check point
where she must slow.

 They will not like her duct-tape mittens
(as if her hands were very cold) but she cannot roll
down the window with her hands stuck at 10 and 2.

Is it very hot inside her womb as she moves
faster down the street we all travel?
Does she cry, "My God, my God!" or merely "Mary!"?

She has ever eschewed the first person pronoun, savoring "I" like
a phosphorescence. It's all the same, isn't it, whether she
is dead before or after impact?

Turn your hands up to heaven.
Let the eyes of your palms, flaccid
as the maws of lilies,
look to those clouds.

What passes there casts shadows
that move away from where they're going
and towards you. ❋

Virgin of Guadeloupe

Nadine May Lewis

for years I didn't trust myself
not enough ...
stopped listening to music
didn't keep candles
there was never any rope
the only knife in the house
a curved serrated blade perfect for vegetables
abominable at meat
even after marriage
even after children ... it took time
feeling is hard,
it is easy to avoid and sometimes necessary
cause feeling is hard
the good the bad every bit of it, feelings are messy
and grief well
grief is quicksand so
yesterday I listen to the radio in my house
for the last month I have been surfing stations in my car
and tonight I lit a candle
the flames shadow pulsating on the ceiling
the virgin of guadeloupe filled us
with the faint scent of roses
and the last of the leaves fell leaving every limb bare
and all those raw emotions crashed down
like so many waves hitting the shore
and I finally just rode it out
let the green leaves yellow
burn crimson and crumple into brown dust ✻

The Angelus, As Mary Heard It   *Rhonda Shary*

> *The human countenance is threatened or even*
> *shattered by the divine countenance, but...the divine*
> *countenance makes us more fully who we are.*
> —LI-YOUNG LEE

> *Every angel is terrifying.*
> —RILKE

"Be not afraid," you said,
and my world stopped
to make way for yours

I was weaving when you arrived
with lilies and the blessing of
incendiary celestial voice

You trembled, sweet messenger
You worried for my fate and my youth,
for the blood river you knew would flow from me

But I have waited all afternoon for you
the shuttle clattering in the quiet:
I have always known my flesh was not my own

I fear nothing

I listen, and wait for God to speak again
in wing-soft works. ✳

Angel

Kappa Waugh

Colleen in our handwork group
is hooking an angel. It's larger
than life, though who knows exactly
the life size of an angel?
In paintings, Gabriel seems about Mary's height,
not so huge she'd get scared and say,
"No, thanks," to so terrifying a prospect
announced by such a frightening visitor.
But this angel, composed of thousand upon
thousand wool loops, is gigantic. Its hands
the size of baseball mitts, its head big as
a large clock face. And that's
without the halo or nimbus — those big,
gold discs that clue you in to the fact that
you're not dealing with the ordinary.
She brings it to the group to work on in sections,
a piecemeal angel. One day she brought
a wing the size of a surfboard.
What will happen when she joins this huge
creature together? Will it rise,
beating its creamy wings and blowing
all our sewing off the table?
Will it cry out, "Be not afraid! I bring
glad tidings," in a voice so loud the
windows shatter, or in such a soft woolen
whisper we only hear it in our hearts? ✳

The Voice
Laura Russo

The path to the old barn is rough and gray like an old man's beard. It begins to inch one way, then quickly changes its mind and straightens out before beginning a steep incline near the base of an enormous oak. It is a road that appears to lead to nowhere, and for this I greatly admire it. In the distance the Catskills loom, blue and magical as they were in Irving's day, perhaps even enhanced by the additions of the modern era. I find nothing more fascinating than the view down the highway to the mall, mountains stark, majestic, the backdrop to a rusty water tower and sagging power lines. They almost seem unreal. But here the backdrop makes more sense. The magic isn't any less intense, but its tune is less interrupted, its power less contrasted.

Sometimes when the wind blows, I can hear a woman's voice in this barn, an odd kind of shouting that is stifled to a whisper. I think if I sit here long enough I may be able to decode her message, and then I may finally understand what has drawn me to such a place. I don't know if the barn is abandoned or if it simply looks unused. There are holes in the walls where the building has been defeated by wind and water, and the roof looks as if the weight of one more crow might cause it to collapse. There are already several perched confidently, watching me as if I were an intruder in their world.

The door creaks loudly when it finally begins to move. It is not nearly as dark inside as I had imagined, there being far more crevices in the roof and walls than I could see from the outside. I take one final look outside to make sure I am alone and see nothing but my shiny silver car sparkling in the sunshine at the bottom of the hill, utterly out of place in such an environment. At first it seems quiet, but the more I listen, the more I am sure that I hear that voice again, the one that had called me in from the road, that had maybe even called me to this road from the highway, sensing I needed something more fulfilling than shopping plazas and chain restaurants in my life.

I sit down gently and squint, trying to adjust my vision to the
dim and dusty light around me so I can better acquaint myself
with this strange place and its even stranger voice. It seems
to hum as I move my head from side to side, up and down,
examining every corner for a sign of life or movement. The place
is utterly still, but the humming persists, becoming louder as my
mind allows itself to perceive it and rids itself of the loudness of
its other thoughts. I have always had trouble quieting my mind, I
realize, and I want to thank the voice for showing me how.

The voice enters my body as it reverberates through the room;
the rhythm of my own movement takes on a element of fluidity
to match the song. It is getting loud in here, I think, and I wonder
if someone were to drive past if they would hear the pounding
rhythm of this voice and see the old barn trembling from the
volume. I, too, am humming, swaying, singing, entirely entranced
by the words I still cannot understand. I know the voice belongs to
a woman, and to this place. This voice could exist nowhere else. Is
it trapped here? Hiding? Or does it belong here where it can relish
in its own loudness, away from everything that renders it inaudible?

Suddenly as I dance freely in the barn a new sound penetrates
the walls. It is distant at first, but slowly becomes dominant,
dulling the voice that drew me here and completely silencing
my own. It blares insistently, calling me back to my life, as if I
had been gone too long. I realize it is my car alarm and scramble
to turn it off, hoping to preserve a bit of the magic I had just
discovered, but it is too late. I decide it must be time to leave, so
I drive away and leave the barn to pass another night on its own.
I wonder how long after I am gone the music will return and if it
will ever be clear to me again. I am headed to my own home, to
the place where the mountains that sing such beautiful songs that
they ring through the tattered walls of old barns, permeating the
land with their fullness, seem like nothing more than a movie
backdrop draped across the horizon. ✳

Who is My Muse?   *Lee Gould*

The lyric soprano, all bosom and alabaster, in her Empire nighty?
the half-shaved tenor, so hairy, so manly
in his glittering armor?

His magic sword shattering
unwomans me. Or
is it Sieglinde?
Fat Wotan swears to punish his errant daughter —

but what's that snaking around my lyre tree?
4 foot 8, bulbous hips, eyes unblinking —
a Rose?
   by another name

Mother —

For crying out loud, imagine
   that Jerk McGee hollering to beat the band,
   who can sleep in all that racket?

but now she sleeps, all knobs and curves and string.
I lie awake. Don't touch it, the air says, it'll break. ❋

Green Tara as Protector
From the Eight Fears
Janet Hamill

Hail Tara   wholly green   of forests deep and emeralds
  lighting the Empire State Building   at Christmastime
  the power of perfect action is with you   as I walk
  down side streets in the dark   the splintered glass
  of trampled vanities   stick with seasoned cares
  to the soles of my shoes

Tara   queen of sacred lore   when the remorseful night
  ends in a taxi   you're waiting in the vestibule   green
  of young sprouts at the botanical garden   jewels
  and trinkets on your arms wide open   hosting yellow birds
  on your shoulders   the satyrs of sidewalk harm
  lay slain   by your arrows

Mother of green processional avenues   at the start
  of the parade   help me follow in your footprints
  five hundred miles between me and the fountain
  on the damping grass in Central Park   green at heart
  green carnations in the flower beds   call me from isolation
  to juggle the planets in my hands

Tara   infinite by virtue of your name alone   protect me
  in moments when everything conspires against me   send
  prayer flags   green of the patina of three-sided daggers
  on the subway   surrounded by an arch of flames   green
  goddess   holding the blue lotus in your hand
  'Homage to you!'

Holy Tara   born of a tear   the Hudson swims with ocean tides
    bearing all losses   your grief is a veil draping
    the George Washington Bridge in a soft rain on the city
    dispersals of shared crescendos transmute   into
    green Moroccan bindings   green pens   and ink
    from your mountain well

Tara red   of henna hands and henna feet   in a corner
    of the room I see you   green with the vigor
    of incandescent lanterns   laughing at every word
    I've ever written   laughing so hard   the doubts
    that hypnotize   vanish   in the spray of green stars
    thrown on the ceiling

Blessed Tara   on a quiet blossom   watching your color
    pour down the sides of tenements   greening
    the pavements   emboldened by wine's forever friendship
    I vow to be made in your image   or all my lifetimes
    show me the way   when I've lost it   lead me
    to the hidden land of snows

Tara   greater than the strength of raptors on the skyscrapers
    bring down   the dust clouds of the firmament upon them
    calm windows on the world   green eyes   ever mindful
    of the gentle   balanced on the edge of a precipice
    green savioress accepting my insecurities as prayers
    say 'Have no fear!' ✳

Edie's Mikveh

Edie Abrams

I bolt the bathroom.
A veil of steam
Engulfs my refuge.
The mirror no longer
Reflects me.

Flickering flame
Can barely be beheld.
A vanilla scent
Secretes round
Each tiny vapor as if
The air waved with
droplets of holy incense.

Tchaikovsky's Fifth.
Steady beats blaze to
Tempestuous timbre.
The music echoes my
Pulsating nerves surely as
Cupid's arrows quiver
'Neath my skin.

Garments ease off.
I free my fettered hair,
Loose it before me so
Locks untangle. I
Penetrate the
Steamy basin.

Buoyant, I think nothing.
Wet hair dozes
On glistening breasts.
Legato notes
Relax my breath.

The day expelled,
My mind
Cleansed from
Le monde's mores,
I immerse.

L'elisir d'amore.
I am a mermaid in metamorphosis.
Botticelli's Venus rebirthed. ❋

And the Sky Opens   *Jeanne Stauffer-Merle*

I am not of the rain.

Rain is the linger the finger-grip
the boat—
the thing that contains and never
the lunge of desire.

I am not of the rain.

Rain is a pool of hand
an inverted hole   lost and lost
in its own beautiful.
It pauses like a tilted head.
It is a bed like that, too.

Listen. This is mine:
These buried tracks. A length of iron.
This unreadable sign propped up like the dead possum
still standing in the middle of the road.
Its leftover eye clings to the skin
like a small black claw or bullet or.

But maybe it's not what I think.
Maybe I'm not of the angled red.
Maybe I am of the frozen—
the rain that sleeps and waits.
Maybe I am of the rain that will not open its mouth
the rain whose throat sings to itself
and closes   as it drowns of its own dream
of rain. ✳

Wet Exit   *Sarah Wyman*

The man held the woman's feet
lovingly to his chest.

As he slept,
down and down she swam
into dark depths
that hid a certain light.

Her legs became a two-lane nameless road away.

Seaweed hair draped on a coral bed,
she remembered the man
only by a clutching warmth in her toes.

Miles high, the man looked down
to see he held a mermaid by the tail,
embellished with a curl of kelp.
Thinking her simply a fish,
mistaking the curve of hip
for a play of waves,
he let go — ❋

PART 2

IDENTITY

Bird of Paradise
(Bird of Paradise quilt top,
1858 – 1863, vicinity of
Albany, New York)   *Suzanne Cleary*

In Albany, New York, circa 1860, no one had seen
the tropical flower named Bird of Paradise,
that orange and violet pinwheel of petals,

the Bird of Paradise quilt depicting birds
of upstate New York, imperfect paradise
of crow, grackle, turkey, a patchwork

quilt of wool and cotton scraps, their dark colors
drawn from bark and nut, from the brief flowers
of a cold place. Do you imagine a farm woman

could work on this quilt for five years
and not be thought a fool,
not ask herself, some nights, *Why?*

Do you imagine that she did not dream of the day
she could be done with it, pull the quilt
over her head, and sleep,

even as she delighted over three linen eggs,
laying them perfectly atop a muslin nest?
Despite the quilt's depiction of actual birds,

do you think that this woman did not understand
bird of paradise as metaphor,
she who lived not far from towns named

Rome, Ithaca, Carthage, Painted Post?
You work with what you are given.
Any farm woman knows this,

knows that paradise, like a bird,
lights on earth for brief moments.
Here, paradise spreads its wings

as a girl's long hair lifts upon the breeze,
or as a blanket floats briefly over,
then upon, summer grass,

bluebells soon to be covered in snow.
If someone brought to this woman's dark parlor
the tropical flower Bird of Paradise, and set it in water,

what do you think she would do?
Do you not think she would sit, and work
by the orange and violet flame of that flower,

its light so like that of a candle,
so like what burned inside of her
as she slid her needle through, back through,

the fabric? For that matter,
weren't they one and the same to her —
a flower, a bird — and both of them

amenable to what she would make of them
in the paradise of her work,
from which she would not fly? ✻

Letters from Riverside   *Carole Bell Ford*

She was feisty and often opinionated, expressed her thoughts
in no uncertain terms. This time, she was going on about how
exasperated she was with the government. But then, resignedly,
said that she expected her opinion to be dismissed as just "a
woman talking politics" since a woman "was only made to keep
the children's faces clean, sew buttons on her husband's shirt
and wash dishes and such." She was indignant that it seemed
impossible for anyone to believe that a woman could choose to
live independently.

　Her remark might easily be taken as a comment by someone
in the mid-1960s. Someone who'd, perhaps, just read Betty
Freidan. But, in fact, it was almost one hundred years before *The
Feminine Mystique.* It was on August 20, 1865 that Esther Howell
sent those words to her closest friend and correspondent, Mary
Stewart. Esther, writing from her home in Riverside, in the town
of Highland, New York, was well aware that, as a woman, she
would be criticized for voicing her opinion about government
policies in post-Bellum American society. "I suppose," she wrote,
"seeing I belong to the femal [sic] sex I might not to open my life
in such a manly Subject ..." Despite her protestations, however,
she didn't hesitate to write about politics, religion, a number of
contemporary social issues, or many other "manly" subjects.

　Esther's letter, from which those quotes are taken, is part
of a collection that was reviewed about ten years ago for the
Huguenot Historical Society of New Paltz, New York, ("Finding
Aid," September 20, 2001) that I'd agreed to read, transcribe and
annotate. It didn't take very long, as I read some of the letters
that had already been transcribed, for me to become fascinated
with this character: a woman who was a product of her time,
whose views were evolving and sometimes contradictory. I
simply wanted to know more about her.

Esther held some radical views for a woman of her social class and milieu. In the letters, in which she comments on "a wide range of subjects, including topics that are rarely discussed in letters written by other local women from this period...." ("Finding Aid," September 20, 2001) she, of course, had a good deal to say about marriage and the role of women in society. (I can imagine that she was influenced by the Seneca Falls Convention; less than twenty years earlier — in 1848 — the rights of women had been eloquently declared there.) And she'd had time to give marriage a lot of thought; Esther was twenty-six in 1865. At a time when women were still being placed in arranged marriages, some as early as the age of fourteen, she was well on her way to becoming a spinster.

Given the fact that she didn't have a very high regard for men, she was probably right to think she would never marry. "What or how is it that I have such a poor opinion of the other sex with some exceptions [?] I think it is their own fault ... men are curious animals." She sorely resented the fact that women were held in low regard: "I wonder if the men dont [sic] feel a sort of humiliation to think that at one period of their valuable lives they actually wore frocks [;] it is a wonder that some of them survive." But she was even less tolerant of women who deprecate their own sex, such as one woman she quotes as saying "the only thing that reconciled her to being a woman was that she would not have to marry one" (August 30, 1865).

Esther is cynical about marriage. She tells her friend, who has come to the defense of the institution, that for every example of a happy marriage Mary can come up with, she can counter with a dozen that are troubled. Esther was not only convinced that she would never marry but clearly seemed determined not to. "I have no idea at present of adding to the misery abounding in this world," she tells Mary (September 27, 1866).

Unless—she found love. With all of her cynicism about marriage, it turns out Esther was a romantic. She hadn't been given to someone in an arranged marriage when she was young and when, she thought, she'd been of a more accepting and pliable disposition. "Perhaps had I married seven or eight years ago ... I might have grown into a sort of content with my lot seeing it was unalterable [.] But now it would be a living death to me to live with a man I did not love (September 27, 1866). Since, however, the opportunities for a mature woman to find someone she could fall in love with were slight she'd, reluctantly, given up on that unlikely scenario: reluctantly, since she admits, "I live at odds to my discretion to never marry. I don't know but what ... woman ever yet lived that naturally would not prefer marriage to single life." And, further, if a man came along that she fell in love with, "I suppose," she muses, "[I] should be just as silly as the rest and all my profound observations are for nothing" (September 27, 1866).

And silly, indeed, she did turn out to be. First, she refers to her beau, coyly, as "a young man of our acquaintance," (Sept. 24, no year but probably 1867). Another reference is more explicit: "The first thing I saw at the ferry was the red whiskers of 'My feller'" (August 3, 1867 or 1868). Then, finally, she comes out with it: "I found father ... alone and I made up my mind I would tell him what was on the carpet. *You* [,] he said as though he did not believe his ears." But it was fine. Her father "never expected to dictate in such matters," she said, "I must choose for myself" (August 3, 1867 or 1868).

In November 1868 Esther was married to Nelson Horton — and they lived happily together thereafter. ✳

Self-Acceptance:
A Hard-Fought Battle   *Nava Atlas*

Some time ago, I kept a cartoon on my bulletin board depicting
two caterpillars creeping along, with a butterfly hovering above
them. One caterpillar eyes the butterfly suspiciously, and says,
"You'll never catch me going up in one of those things!" Maybe it
isn't what the cartoonist intended, but I see it as a metaphor for
the sad state of women's self-esteem. We're destined to become
glorious butterflies, yet we persist in perceiving ourselves
as caterpillars, opting for crawling the safer but less exciting
ground, instead of allowing ourselves to take flight.

It's a tough task to reach the level of self-acceptance that allows
a writer — or any creative individual — to feel she deserves to
let her talent shine, and reap the rewards of her labors. Think of
favorite classic authors such as Edith Wharton, Virginia Woolf, and
Louisa May Alcott, with their distinct styles and personas. It's hard
to imagine that they didn't burst forth with the kind of self-regard
that would allow them to write and succeed gloriously. And yet —
they didn't. Like most of us, they struggled with self-acceptance
for years, sometimes for decades. Consider:

Edith Wharton, a wealthy heiress, was surrounded by
disapproval, from her snooty mother and society friends to her
gadfly husband, who scoffed at her literary pursuits. She tiptoed
haltingly into the world of print, hampered by crippling insecurity.
It took many small victories — published stories, books, and warm
reviews — before Wharton believed she was worthy of success.
Finally she allowed herself to exhale: "The reception of my books
gave me the self-confidence I had so long lacked . . ." It took the
reinforcement of the public and her peers for her to acquire a new
image of herself as a capable, talented author — one who, before
very long, became the first female author to win the Pulitzer Prize
for the Novel in 1921 for *The Age of Innocence*.

Like Edith Wharton, Virginia Woolf's need for approval was vast, and she sought it from her husband, friends, publishers, and critics. But unlike Edith Wharton, those closest to her gave her just that. That didn't allay her constant struggle with self-doubt, seeing herself as somehow "less than." "I can assure you," she wrote to her friend Vita Sackville-West, "all my novels were first-rate before I wrote them." When her publishers or husband praised her efforts, it meant everything to her. Woolf needed the reinforcement of others to build a foundation of self-acceptance, which in turn gave her courage to create works that were experimental and far ahead of their time. Though self-doubt never left her, it was a catalyst to constantly do better, not a signal to stop growing.

Louisa May Alcott was determined to make a living by writing, no small feat for a woman of her time. To support her family, she wrote thrillers, gothics, and "sensational tales" under pseudonyms. After years of toil, she took up her publisher's request to try a "girls' story," and reluctantly cranked out Little Women. Though neither she nor her publisher thought highly of the results, the book became an immediate bestseller. When she learned of its embrace by the public, Alcott changed her tune: "It reads better than I expected. Not a bit sensational, but simple and true ..." No longer going from one anonymous literary identity to another, self-acceptance came after the "simple and true" novel that emerged from the pen of its reluctant author met an enthusiastic audience. Her career blossomed, as did the fortune she had long craved.

Once I learned of the universal struggles of authors like Wharton, Woolf, and Alcott, I realized that I was behaving more like the two caterpillars in the cartoon than the butterfly. I've played it safe by accepting only a certain version of myself as an artist and writer, one that's occasionally at odds with the "real me." It has taken decades, I'm afraid, but that's changing over time, and my mantra is "It's never too late, unless you're dead."

Like the two caterpillars crawling ever so slowly on the ground, the illusion of safety can get in the way of progress. After all, caterpillars are vulnerable to getting smooshed on the road. Sometimes acceptance of a new version of ourselves — as creative beings who have finally arrived, or are just on the cusp of doing so — lags behind what others have already perceived about us: we're already aloft, like the butterfly; we just need the courage to lose sight of the ground below. ❋

Coming Home to Hallelujah   *Carol Yuen Bean*

The topic is hallelujah
and whether after 50 or 70 or 95 years
of particularized suffering
we can yet swallow the bait—
the unexpected light jetting through the tender space
    between the curtains;
the crimson splash on the leathered cheek of an old woman
hauling herself up the steps at the post office;
the neighbor's dog with ball in mouth, his heart straining to
impossible heights at the sight of you;
three men standing on the side of the road gazing up into the
branches of a great white Pine; you stop, your eyes travel up
doubtful, hoping;
the Astor bursting headlong through the crack the mason left in
the long smear of pavement, clinging to its centimeter of soil for
fear of flying away too soon,
the fissure of uncontrolled laughter
the gasp
the tender moan
the scent of green peppers—
that calls us back
to hallelujah. ✳

Saturday Morning:
Meditation on the Soup

Karen Michel

Instead of thinking
about nothing
I thought about the soup.

In breath: the lentils.
Out breath: red beans.

In: add garlic.
Out: chop the rosemary or leave it in sprigs?

In: barley, peppercorns; dried chili from Chimayo.

In: Add the vegetables, leftovers from an art opening.
Out: Trash, transformed into a sultry smell of black olives and
artichokes; cauliflower and broccoli; bits of orange carrot and
hairstrings of celery.

Simmering.
While I
breathe
in and out and in again.

Until
I'm back
to stillness,
to thinking about nothing:
the soup ready; fully cooked. ❋

Three Haiku   *Priscilla Lignori*

restless as the wind
the shirt hanging on the line
by a mere clothespin

so soft to the touch
but harder than my own bones
the weathered beach stone

walking on tiptoe
in the middle of the night
the autumn drizzle ✼

Interpretation: Three Versions   *Mimi Moriarty*

First Version:

In this dream, instead of puppies in the basement I forget to feed
there's an alligator in the yard and even though I've forgotten
to feed him as well, he appears fully grown, possibly having
eaten the puppies in the basement.

The dream ends with a neighbor taking a shovel to its head,
slicing it off with one blow. Dreams collide with reality
so I am stuck with this interpretation. I'm the jury on this one
channeling wisdom from Carl Jung and the voices in my head,

one of them insisting that the alligator is my father, and another
arguing that the alligator is Rush Limbaugh. I'm tapped out.
Can't lift another interpretation from this relentless dream life
that settles over the bed every night.

It's a glimpse into the future, a voice rattles on, a healing
of the past another posits. Let me sleep! I cry out, just
a good night's sleep!

Second Version:

If I continue to forget to feed the pets, and even the invasive
species, what am I not caring for? the soul? the creative life?
my inner child? or maybe this neglect is a mental block,
a psychic block, an emotional block? Then I could ignore it

because the block is there for a reason, or maybe electric shock
treatments would unlock the dream drawer, and hidden behind
the woolen socks would be not the answer but a key that opens
a safe and in that safe would be another key.

This key is not identified so now I have a clue without a new
dream to tell me where the lock is. I take a nap—no dream,
but a chill, a cool thought—it's a key that will open a door
but the door has not yet been hung, the building

has not yet been constructed, the plans have not yet been
drawn, the concept has not yet been imagined. That's a better
interpretation of the dream, don't you think, Carl?

Third Version:

I have attended to the alligator's needs, but I have just forgotten
about it, hence the surprise of the fully grown alligator. This
interpretation is unsettling because loss of memory can be
a crippling affliction even though the loss of dream memories

would afford a productive morning of hoeing or dusting or weaving
or whatever people do in the morning instead of this incessant
journaling. I watch my time but lose it to the alligator and
neighbor with the shovel. What is this dream really about?

Is it about mental blocks, or memory loss, or my father,
or Rush Limbaugh or about losing keys? I feel as though I've run
around this particular dream with unsatisfactory results. It's like
I've pushed a psychic button to the apartment marked 3G.

I'm buzzed into the lobby but there's no elevator, no stairs, so
I'm stuck in the lobby, Carl, just you, me, and the alligator.
He looks hungry, Carl. What shall we do? ❈

Thieves, An Oral Nightmare   *Roberta Gould*

Why did you steal my teeth
when I only wanted to hear the music?
If my mind wandered
did you have to do your trick
make vanish what I'd lived with all my life?

They were performing a Brahms's sonata
one bowing on spiked heels in a sleek red dress
The other one, pudgy, was ultimate heart
at the nine foot grand she sat at
Was it then with your sleight of hand
you snatched my mouth's furniture?

And how I wound up on the train after that
I don't know. It was rush hour, the compartments filled
and I was trapped and forgotten in a corner
unable to chew and hungry
soft and unable to fight

They say be grateful that you still have your eyes
Thank god and your stars and try to behave

Complaints are not needed, it's wartime
And keep your mouth shut, without teeth
you're not very pretty ❋

A Meager Diet of Horizon
from a phrase by Elizabeth Bishop   *Natalie Safir*

The woman contemplating scraps of sustenance
knew how to manage on *a meager diet of horizon;*
the anemic sky offered nothing but boundaries

Winter would not creep upon her unprepared;
shortening days generated watercolor moonscapes,
a rash of recklessness and high wire stunts of amnesia

until she'd settle into the loneliness of it, circle the floor,
a feral animal sniffing out a resting place, wed to a famine
of dailiness, the lack of surprise behind every door ✳

Laid Off Summer   *Carol Graser*

That July the raspberries grew
like slow fireworks, long arcing branches
that tangled into fruit. I scratched
my way to the red globes
ruby princesses, shy
smilers dangling with thorns
It was the over-pruning two years
before that caused the explosion—
that wealth. I'd squat in the wet grass
and peer into brambles, spying
out ripeness, reach in for the light
squeeze that, if ready, pops
them off with no stem. Scarlet
shades piled in the bucket. Those
delicate plumps, those seedy drupelets
I struggled not to complain at abundance
the daily, hot chore of collecting
and storing. I'd pour cold raspberry
sauce over the gray folds of my brain
let the sweet tart soak and stain
flavor me bright red
and less bitter ❋

I Check Their Leaves,
I Water Their Roots...   *Phyllis R. Freeman*

I decided sometime in my late 50s that I needed a hobby. Well,
not really *needed a hobby*. But I did think that my world of going
to the gym (half-heartedly), teaching and conducting behavioral
research (both often with relish), reading (for pleasure), and
interacting with my husband (not necessarily in that order),
seemed limited and unbalanced.

So I set out on a quest.

I had never thought of myself as a collector (except perhaps of
dust from all the housework I have postponed until retirement).
I didn't have an interest in crafts like knitting, or woodworking,
or candle dipping. My childhood music and painting lessons
certainly fanned my life-long passion as a listener/viewer, but not
as a creator. I had always loved flowering things. Why shouldn't I
tackle the most beautiful of plants? I would try to grow orchids.

So I bought one, rescued another, and within several years
had sixty orchids in our small house. I say this with a mixture
of pride and embarrassment the way some multiple cat owners
blushingly admit to the numbers they own. ("And they really
do keep each other company," my cat-loving friends insist.) My
plants line the windows in the dining room, pack three shelves in
the study, and fill the bookcases in our family room.

I am not a good grower. I'm not even a mediocre grower.
Many of my plants have sturdy green leaves but have never spiked
or bloomed. Sometimes in late winter or in early spring our
house is filled with color from those plants I am able to coax into
flowering. White, pink, yellow, brown, and especially varying
depths of purple dominate. The blooms, like flocks of cartoon
moths, flutter in the currents of air from our humidifier, flights
of color and loveliness, heralding a new season. I love the mystery
of not knowing what the flowers will look or even smell like on

new plants. Some will perfume the air with subtle sweetness, others will smell like chocolate, and a few will remind me of wet, musty socks.

I love the challenges of science, skill, and luck involved in growing these living things. I check their leaves, I water their roots, I kill their bugs. As I go about my tasks, I sometimes enter a state that psychologists call "flow." I am wholly engaged in the moment of my actions. For an hour or so each day, when my focus is on the operation of orchid keeping, my breathing slows, I feel energized yet calm, and I am "in the groove." I lose my sense of time and enter something like a Buddhist state of being "at one with things."

I don't claim that orchid keeping is religious or even spiritual. And my "flow" experiences are not daily occurrences. However, when I lose myself, the experience is so enjoyable, I know that cultivating this state more frequently in my daily life would be desirable.

Indeed, tending my orchids can be a metaphor for how to live more fully as I enter "older" age. Perhaps those pressing life decisions that I have postponed won't be so difficult to make after all. Maybe the day will turn out more lovely and calm than I thought it would. Can I tend my life the way I tend my orchids, engaged wholly with my actions in the moment, without worrying about future spikes and failed blooms? Can I rest completely in the present without anxieties about the future or regrets about the past?

All that is, is here now. This moment. These leaves, these roots, and even these bugs. I check, I tend, and I water. I breathe deeply in this moment of being alive. ❋

"Misuse Can Result in Fire or Death by Electrical Shock"

Alison Koffler

After weeks of whining
on my best friend's couch,

I waited until he was out
then stole into what would

have been our new apartment,
past the shadowy, empty

shelves we'd bought from Ikea,
padding down the freshly painted

halls, over the hopeful old floors
we'd scraped and urethaned

golden slick. The cat trotted
after me anxiously, crying

from room to room.
On top of the thrift store armoire

in my pewter picture frame
that horse-faced girl smirked.

Strange dresses were in my closet.
The bathroom was dangerously clean.

I stumbled into an unfamiliar sofa
of designer beige chenille, then quietly

cursed my way to the kitchen
to find the other cat, stretched out

mewing atop the microwave I never
wanted. In a last white room

the rumpled bed stood.
I stuffed some underwear and a bunch

of books into a day pack, and left again,
a bad girlfriend, youthful ex-*hausfrau*,

dragging love's failure like a
raddled banner, not to mention

both cats, stunned to silence,
bumping along in one carrier.

Fifty bucks for my new super
from the ATM, I jam the crumpled

bills into my pocket then cruise
the dollar stores on Lydig Avenue,

maneuvering past other women
in the aisles, fast voices in Spanish

and Albanian. I calculate the cost
of a new life, all the things I might want;

to hitch a ride to Paris or Tangiers,
spot-lit crowds roaring my name,

battalions of lovers scratching at the door,
or maybe quiet, a spiral notebook

an earthenware cup of
Mu tea, a breezy window facing

the Parkway.   Pausing dreamily
among the aisles of scrambled necessities

and plastic junk, I decide, suddenly,
to buy my own extension cord—

fifteen feet long, coiled neatly
and shrink-wrapped, tagged

with repeated warnings of danger
in five different languages—

something to use
that was wholly my own. ※

The Susan Situation   *Lynne Crockett*

I walk daily on the dead-end road where I live, and through these walks I have met quite a few neighbors, usually dog owners who are interested in meeting Rolf, my Standard Poodle and walking companion. One neighbor whose conversations I especially enjoy used to drive by in a Subaru with her old dog hanging out of the window, barking nonstop. The dog made Rolf frantic; he never heard a thirty-mile-an-hour bark before. She stopped once or twice to talk about our dogs and, when her dog died, we spoke for quite a while about her loss. In the fall of 2008, before the presidential election, we shared a conversation that was not dog related. A Republican, she was voting for Obama, her first Democratic vote in fifty years. She listed many reasons why she was abandoning the Republican Party, and, when we parted, I felt that I finally knew her a little better. She had become more than a former dog owner driving a Subaru; she had an identity.

Toward the end of the road lives another neighbor, a friendly woman with an elderly Jack Russell terrier. Rolf loves peeing on the daylilies in front of her house, an act that leads Bodie, the Jack Russell, to bark hysterically through the window. Years ago this neighbor and I introduced ourselves and our dogs to one another. She knows Rolf's name, and I know Bodie's. I can't remember her name. And she calls me Susan.

At first I didn't realize that she was calling me by the wrong name. Maybe I thought she was referring to her sister, who often is with her. I remember turning away after a short chat, raising my hand to wave goodbye, when she called, "Goodbye, Susan!" I looked back, but she already had entered her house. When I next saw her and she again called me Susan, I didn't have the energy to contradict her. Last summer I debated—actually anguished— over whether I should tell her now, after several years of her thinking of me as Susan, that she has been mistaken, that I am

Lynne, not Susan. I became so uncomfortable that I avoided walking by her house, or I chose times when I knew it was unlikely for her to be outside. I became obsessed with "Susan."

But then I began to wonder. Maybe on some level I am Susan. Why not? "Lynne" doesn't even sound like "Susan." There must be some cosmic reason why she calls me Susan. I wondered what my "Susan-like" characteristics were. I thought of all of the Susans I have known to consider what we have in common. Or what we appear to have in common, since there are depths to these women that I can't imagine. This neighbor only knows that I have a black Standard Poodle named Rolf and that I walk on her road. She doesn't know whether I prefer chocolate or toffee, whether I am a teacher or an accountant, whom I voted for (or if I voted at all) in the last presidential election. But she knows that I am Susan. I feel that if I can decipher the mystery of Susan, then I will know something about myself, something beyond the mundane day-to-day facts, something deep and subtle, understood by a few who are outside of me but not grasped by the inside me.

And, of course, I wonder about identity and the creation of identity. If my mother had named me Susan rather than Lynne, would I be different? What rhymes would the kids in grade school have come up with to insult me? What on earth rhymes with "Susan"? Do people treat Susans differently from Lynnes? Does "Susan" carry with it more weight or respect than Lynne? In Mary Gordon's novel, *Pearl,* one of the characters claims that she cannot take seriously a woman named "Lynne." Would this character take "Susan" seriously? How much power does a name have in the creation of others' perceptions of us, of our self-perception?

Now when I walk past this neighbor's house, I become Susan, and I am, somehow, different. I inhabit a new body, a new mind. I feel less weighed down by the petty insecurities that I generally carry with me. Is this because Susan is new to me, so her depths have not yet been exposed? Or is it because Susan is an act, and since I am not really Susan but pretending not to be Lynne, I am not burdened by Susan's issues? Once I turn and head back toward my own house, Lynne returns to inhabit my body, and with her all that is annoying and all that is good. Lynne, however, is still herself mysterious, full of surprises, as are all humans. ❀

Waking at Night   *Amelia B. Winkler*

a distant semi rumbles
the sky is black
across the way
another insomniac paces
lights blazing

once in a summer house
I smelled the salt breeze
off Moriches Bay
watched the curtains dance
heard the mournful bleat
of fog horns even then
I felt there was more
than just this

a rooster's crow wafts
over the rooftops
the air is grey with cooking fires
I lie in bed with a broken ankle
will I get to see the cremation *ghats*
on the Bagmati River
ride an elephant at Chitwan

a clock chimes in the next room
I am a dinner guest near Milton Point
invited to meet an eligible man
all I can talk about is my ex-husband
I cannot remember any names
my host   hostess   the intended suitor
he of the full head of brown hair
how I crave to relive this scene
given who I have become ❋

What I Save   *Catharine Clarke*

I save sentences
and book titles that I want to read.
I save addresses of interesting people I've met.
I save plastic produce bags, twist ties, and rubber bands.
I save every write-up of my daughters' performances,
    every doodle my mother has drawn,
        every greeting card that says "I love you."
I save seeds, even when they're packed for a previous year.
I can't bear to toss out Monhegan poppies,
    sweet peas, freesia never bloomed.
I save chipped, cracked plates
    to catch water under my houseplants.
I save china I never eat from, fabric I never sew,
    needlepoint I never finish.
I save memories of sawdust floors;
    red, black and yellow rings around corn snakes:
red touch yellow, kill a fellow, red touch black, venom lack.
I save Hurricane Donna winds,
    squeaking mice in my doll house,
Daddy Long Legs crawling up the wall over my bed.
I save the golden flax of my grandmother's braids,
the smell of talc and Pond's cold cream,
her shuffle and scuff across the wood floor.
I save Beatles songs,
every sung word in "The Sound of Music"
and "The Wizard of Oz," my munchkin voice singing
"follow the yellow brick road".
I save dreams of high grass, an open turquoise sea,
a red-winged black bird in winter,
a kiss that never came, a letter that did.
I save little girls' snowsuits needing elastic

and Oshkosh overalls missing one clasp.
I save these in a box marked "Things to be Mended,"
   a box moved seven times in 21 years.
I save poems I wish I'd written,
   pieces of poems I wish I hadn't.
I save years of sorrow hidden in a cupboard in the cellar
   waiting to be found.
I save grief because I believe in joy; I save joy
   because I know there will be grief.
I save this moment, and this one, and this.... ❅

Duck Pond in Tuckahoe

Adrienne Hernandez

she sits on a bench dedicated
to someone's beloved wife
(perhaps her own)
as ducks swim in pairs
geese squawk
a commuter train roars
like a wounded elk
and birds become bats

as night falls
the black lab at her feet
knows the futility of waiting
keeps this to himself ❋

Grace
For Tanya   *Rachael Z. Ikins*

Umbrella folds of squash leaves
moulder like an old man's coat hung too many
years on the cellar door hook.
Tomato vines snake out of their cages
as if to escape, green skeletons grip grass carpet
along an outer bank.

Cocooned against squirrels with chicken wire,
one anemic eggplant refused to grow.
The last bus that finishes the day, bluejays blast
in after yellow clouds of finches. You can
tell the season by the birds, spring orchestra
silenced, replaced by riotous cricket competitions
each lengthening night after sun sinks into the swamp.
Sunlight so bright white, my surprised eyes water
as I flip flop through the garage to walk the dogs.

Yes, red bounty simmers on the stove. Summer — boiled,
blanched and skinned. Shredded fine and mixed
in a large stock pot. Herbal fragrance fingers the air,
carries memories' burst basket, juice drooled beneath. Ice,
blizzard flow behind hurricanes' swirling skirts. Nobody
    but an unknown
poet thinks of this. Crowds cross the fairgrounds,
munch fried dough, sausage sandwiches, swill over-priced
beer, wine, gawk at swine, exotic chickens, horses, humiliated,
hooded birds of prey. Cigarette smoke, grandstand music, sweat

reach high above the ferris wheel, the tilt-a-whirl,
nausea on a roller coaster as it dives upside down
into darkness, into midnight. Winter waits. This glorious
burnished gold, purple, magenta day, a mouse creeping along
the baseboard only but for the grace of a white cat. ❋

Egypt Beach, Massachusetts

Pauline Uchmanowicz

A pre-swimmer practices
dead man's float, plays

duck-duck-goose, then
after lessons she drifts

back to the family
towels and umbrella,

where on his fingertip
her father spins a ball

as precisely as a planet
homes into syzygy,

the girl's attention poised
on the frontier that separates

matter from logic. Edging
toward the orb, head arced

with limbs stretched wide,
the child forms a five-

pointed starfish — she could
wish upon her own body

for mastery of flutter kick
and arm-over-arm crawl.

A flea pushes around a granule.
Time presses against nets. ❋

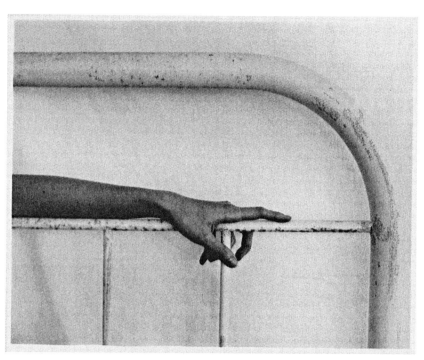

PART 3

GENDER and the BODY

Hudson, NY—1960   *Tana Miller*

I stalled my mother's big
tank of a fifty's car
on the train tracks
that crossed the main street
in the stupefied town
where I grew up,
heard a train whistle,
just in time;
an inexperienced driver,
a foolish teenager,
a near miss,
a close call.

Or did I, barely sixteen,
a disparate collection of hair and bones
and broken, broken heart,
brake on the tracks,
as deliberately as I had worn
my favorite blue dress
cinched tight at the waist
although I was going nowhere
nowhere at all?
Did I turn off the ignition,
and stare out of the De Soto's windows,
expressionless, even when I heard
the freight train's whistle?
At the last, last minute
did I change my mind?
Have all these years
justified that engine's coughing
and protesting, that haunted girl's

shaking foot lifting
from the clutch,
that lurching forward,
that thundering, screaming disappointment? ❋

Thirteen   *Alyssa Fane*

Running into the darkness, I felt his presence invading, deceiving my mind. Behind the curtains of our high school's stage, I lost the most precious part of my innocence. Frederick was tall, red-headed and freckled, but not the boy you'd imagine. Through his thick glasses one would not find a bookish young man, but a boy: obnoxious, loud, perverse.

I emerged from the curtains with a mixture of regret, excitement, and agonizing pain. Up the antique stone steps and out the door into the spring air—I walked home.

From then on there were sessions of love-making, or more accurately, my blind submission. We hid, we ran, we laughed, we discovered. It was my own little secret from my other life. I needed him, I felt.

I became reckless. After school we'd sneak into the library, the basement, anywhere we could be alone. Not getting caught made me feel invincible. My affair made me feel important, for the first time in a long time.

Eventually I was discovered.

I was thrown into the cage of a starving grizzly, who had been eyeing me for years. My stepmother, Judy, cornered me, demeaned me more than I'd already demeaned myself. I had already been sneaking around with Frederick, and she didn't like him. I was harshly told that "the apple didn't fall far from the tree," that "I'd better not get knocked-up," and that she "will not allow me to have children." The sole option I had if I were to become pregnant became clear as she held me close enough to spray saliva on my face with every violent threat. Her big dark eyes, dark hair, and giant body always scared me as a child, but my fear multiplied when she became angry.

I could never escape my absent mother's misdeeds: "the slut," "the crazy one," "the reckless." Already I was deemed the "bad apple," but now I was branded.

Our relationship continued.

The abuse at home was too hard for me to endure. Forbidden from the kitchen, I "stole" food when no one watched, or starved when I missed a meal. I recall being burnt in the shower from a cold faucet running downstairs—five minutes was apparently too long. The phone? Forbidden as well. It was "her," Judy's, house, and she could "do whatever [she] wanted" in her house and to me. "I can't wait for you to move out so I can have my family." I heard these words almost every day. I channeled this hate I felt and endured into what my young mind thought was love. I had found a vice in him.

He made promises: marriage, children, happiness. I was enthralled with him. What a new world awaited me!

We found time to see each other through the barriers my stepmother set.

Walking the dog gave me a daily excuse to leave the house. These were one of the best and easiest ways to see him. We'd meet by a small bridge over the stream right outside of town. We would look into the water, seeing the distorted image of ourselves in the trickling stream. Only talking occurred on those visits.

Other times our contact was less innocent. I never told him "no."

I began to sneak him over. Early in the mornings, after my father and Judy had left for work, and before my two little sisters awoke, he would sneak up to my bedroom. It became a troubling habit, and eventually we elongated his stays. I'd go outside after I put the girls in front of a movie to join him in the garage. He'd be waiting, smoking a cigarette when I'd appear pajamaed and ready.

In an old, domed, wicker chair, I'd lose myself in him. I was always frightened. It was often dark and cold. The atmosphere combined with my innate discomfort made for unpleasant encounters, yet I found them satisfying in an unsettling way.

I wasn't a burden to everyone; somebody wanted me. ❋

Devil's Paintbrush Mountain   *Georganna Millman*

My plan of escape includes
the summer math of attraction.
In this heat, my brothers won't look
for us clear above the tree-line.
They think I'm too young to know
lovers meet at Rattlesnake Ledge.
You slip on flint and slate.
Your pacing riles low scrub flowers.
Scented pollen sticks to your sweat.
By the time I meet you, I am a vision.
You can't take your eyes off me.
You are as skinny as a stalk.
With the jack-knife I stole from home
I swear on abundant two-tone blood
petals that I will make you forget
the life in town you had before me.
You are the boy my parents hate.
I touch the scar on your knee
with my tongue because no girl
has thought of doing that to you. ❉

The Apples of Discord   *Carol Goodman*

Every year when the apple blossoms bloom the town council of
Discord selects a Queen of the Apple Blossom Festival. Apples
are a big deal in Discord. They're our primary agricultural
product and the town's favorite symbol. We eat our Sunday
dinners at the Apple-a-Day Diner, buy our pies at the Honeycrisp
Pie Company, and we all went to Lil' Blossoms Preschool. Our
high school's mascot is Johnny Appleseed. For many years the
basketball team was called the Redskins, but for obvious reasons
that was changed to the Johnny's back in the seventies, which
isn't much better if you ask me, but then, no one does. Apple
orchards ring the town like a moat protecting us from the evils
of the outside world — or at least the *city people* who summer in
Eden, the town just south of us along the Hudson.

Discord separated from the town of Eden after the Apple
Blossom Festival in 1893. The festival was held early that year
because an unusually warm spring had forced the apple blossoms
into bloom. Liza Mallon was Queen. There's a picture hanging
in the library, back behind the romance novels, of Liza all decked
out as Blossom Queen in a Grecian dress, her long blond hair
hanging loose to her waist, as Junius Swann lays an apple blossom
wreath upon her head. You can tell just how beautiful she is by
the expression on Junius Swann's face. He would have been about
thirty then, already on his way to becoming one of the richest
men in America. He's looking at Liza as if he wants to snatch her
up. Which is what he did — just a few hours after this picture was
taken. While the farmers sat around drinking last year's hard cider
and talking about this year's crop and the farmers's wives drank
tea and lemonade and talked about whose pie would win the apple
pie contest in the fall, Junius Swann was telling Liza that she was
far too pretty to be a farmer's wife even though she was engaged
to marry Amos Tyne. He told her about his house on Fifth Avenue

and the one in Newport and about how he would take his bride on a honeymoon trip to London, Paris and Rome—not a weekend in Niagara Falls. He fed her fresh strawberries from the Swann Court greenhouses, which must have seemed like a miracle to a farmer's daughter who knew it would be another month before the strawberries ripened in her father's fields. Rich men have no need to wait on the season for their fruit to ripen, he might have told her. But he probably just needed the familiar old lies to sweep her off her dainty feet. While the farmers drowsed under the heavy, bee-drunk blossoms, they slipped away in Junius's cabriolet back to Swann Court.

In the morning, when Silas Mallon's wife told him that Liza had not come home after the festival and that she wasn't with her fiancé either, Silas drove his cart up the long drive to Swann Court. When the butler told him that Mr. Swann was not in he only said he would wait and stood on the marble steps, hat in hand, while the sun climbed high in the sky and made the whole marble mansion glitter. With his farmer's eyes he might have looked across the river and seen storm clouds gathering over the Catskill mountains and seen a late frost coming to ruin his apple crops. He might have been thinking about young buds forced into bloom too fast by deceptive warm breezes. He might have been figuring how he could cut his losses when Junius Swann finally appeared at noon in a silk dressing gown, smelling of liquor and apple blossoms. Liza snuck out onto the second floor landing and crouched beneath the Tiffany glass windows of a swan and a girl. She expected loud voices, so when instead her father and her lover spoke in whispers she stole down to hear what was being said. Somewhere on those marble steps she must have heard Junius offer her father recompense for the daughter stolen. So many acres for a despoiled virgin, cash promised against this year's crop no matter what its yield.

I imagine her riding back in her father's cart down River Road, hair tangled with wilting blossoms, her father's rough

wool coat over her bare shoulders. The temperature had already
begun to drop. By nightfall icy rain was falling on the orchards,
glazing each bough and bud with a sheath of ice. I imagine
that to Liza Mallon the boughs cracking sounded like her life
shattering into a million pieces.

By the morning the apple crop for that year had been
destroyed. The smaller farmers were ruined, but not Silas
Mallon. He'd made his deal with Junius Swann and had enough
money not only to survive, but to buy up the smaller farms,
including the Tyne's. He gave the Tynes back the lease, though,
as Liza's dowry when she wed Amos Tyne in July. She wore a
dress the color of apple blossoms, loose enough to hide her belly.
Silas even paid for the couple to have their honeymoon in Niagara
Falls, and he paid for the pretty new house they moved into when
they came back. He himself carved the two cradles out of apple
wood when Liza was delivered of twins. And he paid for the
coffin to bury Liza after she was found the next spring hanging
from an apple tree that had just begun to bloom.

The next year Silas Mallon led a group of farmers in their
secession from the town of Eden. They named the new town
Discord. You'd think the town elders would have objected to the
name, but by then Silas Mallon was so rich that no one could object
to any fancy he took—not even his insistence that a new Apple
Blossom Festival be held each year with a new Queen crowned.

"What more bad could happen because of it?" he was once
overheard to say. ❀

The Mice, The Barn, and The Red Scare

Abigail Nadell Robin

When I was fourteen, I felt like a hermaphrodite, waiting to be taken by one gender or another. I thought that the twenty-two year old summer camp horseback riding instructor was cute. I fondly remember how he taught me to ride bareback in the small lake in Kent, Connecticut. He chose an old swayback mare, gently lifted me onto her and led us into the lake, surrounded by tall, straight pines, stubby blue spruce and shaggy hickory trees. The lake surface glistened and offered comfort and safety. Joy encompassed me. I was away from the ugly, brick Bronx walls, my suffocating parents, and my awful American History teacher, Mr. Fink.

Little did I realize at that time the repressive nature of the silent frustrating 50s, where speech was curbed and psychological suppression reigned supreme. I was sick and tired of hearing his favorite litanies: "I like Ike … I take the fifth." Fink bored the hell out of me. He was a broken record. I never took notes; instead, I watched him fondle his crotch and then take his fingers to his nose and smell whatever scent existed below his chino pants.

I stood in front of the camp's long bunk mirror, angry, anxious and painfully anonymous. Why did I look like a boy? Why was my chest so flat? I felt like a midget with broad shoulders, and to boot, my camp counselors, Mimi and Lois, put a bowl over my head and styled my hair in a Buster Brown cut. They tempted me, physically, but they reminded me of Mr. Fink playing with his crotch. I couldn't make sense of their brand of petting each other; I was uncomfortable with their attention.

I missed being back in the Bronx; here, in summer camp, I had to make new friends. I missed my old friends I had during the school year. We all hung out in my three-room apartment, because I was the only latchkey kid on the block. We'd watch the soap opera, "The Edge of Night," and we'd play doctor, exploring each other's bodies while viewing my father's deck of pornographic playing cards hidden in the top drawer of his dresser.

One hot, steamy afternoon in early August, the riding instructor took me into the lake again; we rode bareback together on a frisky Palomino. I held my arms around the riding instructor's stomach, feeling his developed and hardened muscles and smelling his sweet and sour scent, which mingled with the smells of the rotting forest. We came out of the lake electrified—prancing like the Palomino. We headed towards the red barn. I looked at him, and what I beheld frightened and thrilled me. There was a big bulge in his black-watch plaid swimming trunks. I wanted to be anywhere else than heading toward the looming red barn. I wanted safety—home—the red brick walls in my Bronx, where my parents suffocated me.

A steaming five-foot high pile of horse manure sat next to the barn door. Its scent was sweet and sour like his, and it made my head spin. He instructed me to put the horse in his stall and to take off the bridle and reins, which I did. I then took a moment to look closely at him. He was not a big man. As a matter of fact, he was only a few inches taller that I was. His funky blonde crew cut and his Sinatra blue eyes took my voice away.

We stood eye to eye—bright blue to dark brown. He took my hands in his, and roughly pulled me away from the fodder. He pushed me up against the peeling paint, then kissed me hard while tenderly rubbing my face. I watched him pull down is plaid swimming trunks. I remember thinking, "Gee, his penis has a fold hanging over the tip." I stared at it, and my vision faded as if a great fog had rolled in. I felt his gentle tug on the bottom of my bathing suit and watched his penis stand up and salute my vagina. I opened my legs to salute his grand entrance. He pumped and pushed and finally exploded. Afterwards, he leaned his head on my shoulder and shuddered. I struggled to get out from under his weight, and I finally pushed him off. I felt as if my lungs were collapsing and my head was about to implode. I ran like a coyote back to the safety of my bunk.

None of my bunkmates were there, but I didn't give a damn where they were. I had to take care of myself — Be Careful. I ripped off my bathing suit bottom and ran into the shower room. A pink, sticky stain covered my crotch. I dropped the bottom into the sink, turned on the hot faucet and scrubbed at the stain. What had I done? I thought of Lady Macbeth, but I hadn't stained my hands with anyone's blood. I had only been curious.

I yearned for my mother and knew that she would understand. I remember the years before summer camp when she sat me down in the kitchen after coming home from work all day as a bookkeeper in the garment center. She had bought me a book: *A Child Is Born*. I remember thinking that I was hurting her feelings when she tried to instruct me about sex. I said something like, "I know all about that stuff, don't bother me."

Standing in front of the bunk mirror, I heard her cautioning voice. "Honey, the stain is to remind you to be careful." I turned on only the hot water in the shower and fiercely washed myself, as if the hottest water I could stand would change the intensity of the experience. I scrubbed the inside of my vagina and made it raw in order to make sure that the stain would not remain. I wrapped myself in a towel that my mother bought me to take to camp. It smelled new and fresh and clean — the way I thought my mother imagined me.

I remember playing the role in *Spoon River Anthology* of Amanda Baker who moaned, "Henry got me with child/knowing full well/I would lose my life giving birth to this."

Nobody was going to get me with child, I thought as I came out of the shower. Curiosity would not kill this cat. And then, fear gripped me; I threw the towel across the room and ran like a feral cat from the shower room to my bunk dresser for clean, white underwear, which my mother made sure I had.

The drawers were stuck, swelling with the humidity. I struggled, terrified, wishing I was dead. So much darkness and dank filled the air. As I struggled, rays of light began to move into the room; they reflected off the mirror. I was aware and in awe of myself and asked: Who was I? Who would I become?

The drawer opened and six mice scurried about building their nests. I was now a woman but was certain that I was not ready to build any kind of nest. ✻

Nothing Is Cool   *Maryann Hotvedt*

Started upstate along
arrowhead hudson
after school snow-cones
and holy ways
left it though
for a west coast dream
while the eucalyptus clicked
and springsteen rehearsed
i visited whole earth stewart
who hangs in sausalito but
drives a land rover anyway
so i tailgate pickups north
war weary like twain
to calaveras and more tall tales
hitched to seattle but
right from the start
nirvana saw it coming
cashed-out californians
wearing pricey jeans
torn at the knee
picked up 80 east
sang taylor songs
from stockbridge back
to boston's bronze revere
looking for the citgo sign
just as drunk but without you
90 to the thruway while
springsteen hits the garden

and explains the pain
the east can't shake
and me wishing
ron howard was bent over
my california dreaming script
a start-up story in a garage
rags to riches to rags
because i haven't been able
to follow it up with anything
that cool since. ❊

Smoking Gun

Mala Hoffman

I smell it everywhere.
In the bathroom
after you've brushed
your teeth,
in the undercurrents
of your perfume,
the folds of your
black down jacket.
I even smell it on me.
The crook of my hand,
between thumb
and forefinger.
I sniff myself
while driving
and sometimes
I imagine it on my breath,
as though it was
me,
again,
rolling tobacco so tightly
that the cop
who stopped you
had to slit it open
just to discard the paper trail. ❊

Embodied   *Carolyn Quimby*

Looking back at photos from elementary school, I sometimes can't believe that I am the girl who is wearing my face in those pictures. It is obvious that girl has yet to feel the first pangs of self-consciousness; she looks genuinely happy. Her mouth is all spaces and gaps and haphazardly placed teeth, but she is smiling. She has her arms wrapped around her best friend so tightly that they look like one person. I can't help but notice the fullness of her freckled face and the soft rolls of her stomach, and one word comes to mind before all the others: fat. Not youthful, beautiful, or talented, but fat.

※ ※ ※

The first time I remember having a negative reaction to the way I looked was in the third grade. My best friends at the time were all gathered on lounge chairs around Montana's enormous in-ground pool. They casually passed the Banana Boat SPF 8 Tanning Oil to each other. Our goals for the summer were to have the perfect trampoline-fort sleepover and achieve the deepest tan possible.

Kayla, blonde, blue-eyed, and see-her-ribs thin, spread the oil across her beauty mark speckled stomach. The sun took to her immediately. I stared down at the dark pink Speedo stretched across my stomach; the soft, white expanse of my thighs; felt the sweat gathering along my hairline. Montana passed the bottle to me with a knowing smirk.

"You look like spilt milk," she laughed.

I forced myself to laugh, spraying my legs (twice) before placing the bottle onto the cement. Montana turned onto her stomach and closed her eyes. I stared at the dimples in her back and tried to find my own; I couldn't. We rotated ourselves all afternoon.

That night, I examined myself in Montana's bathroom mirror. I searched for the golden brown color we had been chasing all day, but instead only found the pink bloom of sunburn. I lifted my shirt, searching my body from all angles. My stomach was as white as ever.

※ ※ ※

Would you still be my friend if I looked like this? I asked Montana. We were curled up on her queen-sized bed, the thick maroon comforter pulled up to our chins. My face was contorted into a monstrous grimace complete with crossed eyes and tongue hanging out of my mouth.

No, she told me, honestly and without hesitation.

This was a game we played often. For girls not even ten years old, we were completely obsessed with the way we looked. We were always aware that, if you looked hard enough, mirrors could be found anywhere: car windows, vases, the brass knobs on the four posters of her bed frame, and, even, each other. Montana would be the first person to tell me if my hair was sticking up or if my breath smelled bad. She was beautiful. Her chocolate brown hair was long and wavy. She had long dark eye lashes that lined her huge brown eyes. Her skin was the color of milky coffee. The most vivid memories I have of Montana are of us are in her bed, peering into the brassy knobs, and laughing at the way our faces distorted. We would laugh at the chipmunk-cheeked girls staring back at us until it wasn't funny anyway. One of us would pull away from the tiny fun house mirrors as if coming up from underwater, clutching our cheeks for dear life, making sure they had never really grown in the first place.

Would you still be my friend if I looked like this? No. Yes. No. Definitely not. We would ask each other the same question over and over and over until the weight of all our fake deformities and abnormalities lulled us to sleep. In the morning, we would start all over again. It never stopped. It still hasn't. ※

Try Attaching Sensation to the Figure in Memory

Karen Neuberg

"Try being a figure in memory"
—Carmen Giménez Smith,
"Photo of a Girl on a Beach"

Try figuring out whether memory
hibernates in the cave at the end of the beach
or in the hovel where a family prays over bread,
or the mansion surrounded by gardens & lanterns
that shine through night's shadows hovering at dusk.
Then try to slake your way through density
into the soft call touching you now, luring you
with surface ease — kisses
barely grazing your lips, caresses on layers
of time. Try being that figure who lays herself
across desire, or the one before who waits
for desire to arrive. Or the one prior, she
who hears the word desire for the first time
and uses it to attach stars to her body;

and then try to remember what it feels like
the first time she falls — ❈

In the Women's Locker Room   *Sally Bliumis-Dunn*

Over the tops of the lockers,
I hear a woman

talking, talking.
Just the trail of her sentences,

sentencing,
sentencing her listener

to the silence of a tree.
While she, like an animal

nose to the ground,
follows the trail

of her own words, her scent.
Tense, she is on the prowl:

she is talking about
her body, her body.

She can't decide
if she wants to be

fat with no wrinkles,
or skinny with wrinkles.

But for now, she says
she just wants to keep

her muscles in tone:
her muscles intone to her:

"Be somebody;
Be some body." ※

Waiting Room for a Mammogram   *Alice Feeley*

An unlikely herd propped up sharply
in chairs along one wall,
we women hold clipboards of old questions,
repeat what we can remember,
listen for our names.

Faces are strained, someone holds her head.
Another's foot is tapping in the air.
She scans her third magazine.
Uniformed staff come and go without a word.
Tight voices ask, "How long?"
"Is this the right place?"
A name is called, repeated.
Everyone looks, but no one answers.

On TV an exuberant chef
cuts up peppers, talks, smiles, talks.
There's squirming in the seats.
Eyes framed with ringlets of strawberry blonde
look blankly at *The Times* front page.
Somali child, starved and dead,
lies at its mother's breast
nameless for all the world to see.

Eventually, our names are called. Imaging,
excruciating. Then all is finished but the wait
for phone or letter. TV cooking continues
above a wastebasket holding *The Times* discarded.
April begins

and they still hang on with no life left,
these wide maple leaves gone brown,
turned in on themselves
like crumpled paper.
Unmoved by winter
they still shudder on thin stems
above soft ground
where other leaves
are turning into earth again.
A few yards away a gold sign
blows against a telephone pole.
"On Sunday," it says
"we will be selling our home
to the highest bidder."
And across the bare landscape
a magnolia teases thirty degree night air
with dense buds ready and rosy pink. ❃

Naming the Scar   *Judith Prest*

some scars are visible
   red slash across the chest
   white ladder running up a cheek,
   purple train tracks from collarbone
   to belly button mapping a
   chest cracked open to
   fix a broken heart

my scars run through every nerve:
   panic and paralysis
   hair on the back of my neck
   goes up, breathing
   becomes difficult,
   every muscle clenches

naming the scar
   alters everything
   to name it is to re-draw
   boundaries between
   before and after.
   broken and whole:
naming my scars shatters
the victim shell ❋

Mentally Awaiting Menopause   *Teresa Marta Costa*

Mentally awaiting menopause
red clouds engulf
enlighten
&
enrich
my well being.
Maybe just a
stuck egg
a pocket full
of gas
Or
maybe I just
never treated
my period
like
The Great Goddess

    I should 've taken
    her out to dinner...... ❀

What You Will Believe

Irene O'Garden

The orange you will believe in, and her love.
Your mother's fingers peel its shimmer skin,
spritzing citrus cross your nose, and in
your eye, so that you could not see — above

and then upon you — a single stinging tear
obscures what you will never now believe:
the whole upended ocean in a heave
drowning, drowning all you know. What you called here

is smashed to silt; what you called her
the gushing salt erased, but for that final taste,
that segment of sweet orange she passed —
her parting gift: distraction and the blur.

All we love becomes debris.
You. Me. Why fight the battering?
We're not made of matter, but of mattering,
Love answers, turns and tends catastrophe. ❀

Dead Shot
For Venus Ramsey, Miss America 1944   *Barbara Adams*

Eyes blue as the Mediterranean
On a summer afternoon,
Lips tasting of salt and honey,

A bosom men cannot keep their hands off,
Like squeezing ripe melons
But worth the slap.

Belly button, for God's sake!
What did you think,
I was born from a clamshell?

I had seafoam hair,
Silky skin and earthy breath,
A heathen love potion

Mars drank, and lost the war
Filling me with his seed
To make blind Eros.

How many were there?
Gods and men
Having their fun then gone.

Now I'm a grandmother
Stooped over a walker,
A crone no one recognizes.

Who would believe it was me?
Breasts sagging under a baggy sweater,
Snarly gray hair, skin stiff as shoe leather,

My famous wide hips worn flat,
Flabby and barren
From love-making on hard ground.

Now I love living alone
Enjoying the fruits of my labor,
In a house without mirrors.

Until a teenaged crook broke in
Stealing my silver memories,
Gold statuettes of my beauty.

Wheels squealed in the getaway van.
I dropped my cane and drew my pistol
From my apron pocket
And shot out the bastard's tires —
Venus still has perfect aim!
"Ha!" I yelled, calling 911 on my cell phone.

"I'm trying to live a peaceful life
And all I get is
One damned man after another."

"Just another old bag," says the cop,
His hand fondling my figurine,
His other copping a feel of my butt.

It never ends — ☀

Pull

Penny Freel

Details of memories are funny things. What you swear really did happen and is the honest-to-god truth, too often becomes a smear of what was once a crystal clear moment. I hope I tell it the same way I did nine years ago.

I was six when my Aunt Dee started competing in skeet shooting contests. We were all black-haired, brown-eyed, dark complexioned, but Dee was petite and small-boned and blue-eyed, like the robin's egg I found cracked on our front sidewalk when I had just turned five. Aunt Dee's hair was lighter too: a wispy ash brown she pinned up in a bun so tight it pulled at the corners of her eyes. Dee made a point of always dressing up when she would take her daily walk. *Mop*, she would say, *pay attention. The outside is just as important as the inside.* I sat on her bed and watched as she gently eased up each silk stocking with the pencil point black line that would snake up the back of each leg.

She slipped her feet into her black and white patent leather shoes, pulled from her closet a blue dress, usually with tiny pearl buttons to match the pearls around her neck, reached up to the top shelf of the closet to take down her small veiled hat and bobby pinned it to her head, and after inspecting her white gloves, she would unlatch and pull open the front door of her house. Every day for almost a year, she carried a picnic basket lunch with her. She would pass my parents' Main Street house, directly across from the rectory porch, nod without smiling to Father Brian, who sat and sipped his late morning scotch (who my mother said should have kept his goddamn mouth shut), and past the liquor and candy stores my uncles and father owned. Some grown-ups said Dee had airs, and shouldn't have, considering what happened. I did not know what airs meant. *Mop,* my aunt would declare in her soft voice, *I refuse to remain unnoticed.* My aunt would make her solitary walk with shoulders set and eyes forward.

It was summery warm on that October day when we drove out on old route 55 to watch my aunt compete. Dee had on her fringed Annie Oakley jacket and had traded her blue dress and silk stockings for trousers and boots. *Mop, pay attention now.* Ava Ann, my mother, with my baby sister riding her hip, my older sister twined around the other, yelled over to my aunt, *Send her back if she gets in the way*, and then her brown eyes hardened and narrowed behind her butterfly rims when she glanced over to where my father and my uncle lounged against the red and white '57 Mercury. Their arms were draped around each other's shoulders as they nursed their Rheingolds, pulled on their Camels, leaned in to laugh. My father was handsome, but my Uncle Tony was something else, my mother grudgingly had said, and I think Auntie Ella had told my mother she didn't trust her husband around him too much. Poodle skirted black and white saddle shoed teenagers, who giggled and circled my father and uncle like honey bees, made it a certainty that my mother would later pull open the car door to begin the ride home with *God damn it.* My uncle Tony had disappeared for awhile, but before his absence had time to settle in and become more than an dull longing, he was back — his familiar footsteps on the front porch, the two bits knock, *Hey there Mop*, scooping me up in his arms, *How are you, sweet bee? Ava Ann? Is my brother home?*

Pull! Aunt Dee called as she swung her '54 Premier Skeet L.C. Smith up and followed the arc of the clay and Bam! Bam! A pair of doubles at station 7. *Tony*, aunt Dee called, *Honey, did you see? Tony? Tony? Anthony?* He finally looked up and over. *I sure did; you're a deadeye, darling. One more, Tony, one more.* My uncle waved and then went back to whispering into my father's ear. The honeybees continued to buzz and swarm. I held on to the suede fringes of my aunt's jacket as she moved to station eight. *Mop, are you paying attention? Keep your eyes open. Hold your breath. Count. Aim. Pull!* Aunt Dee's rifle came up, an extension of her left arm, and just as it was beginning its ascent, before I had even counted to two, my aunt's ivory sight and nitro-barrel, for a half beat, were dead centered on my uncle's heart. ❈

Seminole Hard Rock   *Sari Grandstaff*

We ended up at the Seminole
Hard Rock Casino
shortly after Anna Nicole Smith
died there
and as we walked among
the fire eaters
our mouths agape
I couldn't help wondering
about whether the tans
were real or fake
whether the hair was
extensions or an actual wig.

We were there for the death of an uncle
to put his condo up for sale
to meet a person
for the first time
claiming to be a relative
to whom half the condo was left
the condo near the dog track
and the Indian casino resort
where Anna Nicole Smith
also died
also alone. ✻

the woman who buys
her own diamonds

Judith Kerman

buys at auction
the auctioneer bawling his price his price his price
an antiques dealer
bidding against her from the back row

listens to the frogs chime
from a nearby marsh
but she's over forty

hopes but does not believe
does not take herself lightly

tilts the stones in sunlight, watches
the sparkles splash across her shirt
as she drives, ring hand on the wheel

wears it on her middle finger
so there's no mistake ❀

Housewife Sheds Her Skin Like a Snake

Judith Saunders

It was easy.
She felt herself loosening
at the edges, a slight flaking
of the toes and fingers, an itching
in the corners of the eyes.
Working gently from the navel
she peeled the skin off her torso
in one smooth, translucent coil,
lifted the facial epidermis
almost intact, a shredding mask,
pulled from her extremities
long strips of scaling tissue,
simple as shedding a sunburn.
From the final, tickling tatters
she wriggled free, born-again baby. ✳

Portrait of a Woman with Windex   *Ann Lauinger*

A semi-circle of crumpled pages,
Blurred and soggy, garlands the foot
Of the ladder where she stands like Venus
Rising from the foam, or like some
Shepherdess in an old poem, greenly
Eminent amid amorous posies.

Except that she is washing windows:
Old news blackens her hands.
So crime rubs out grime, pain
Cleanses pane, and there is a solvent,
If not a solution, for the old Globe
In troubled Times. Circling the squares,

Listening for the squeak of *clean*,
She ponders the way, under pressure,
Some life becomes diamond, but most
Becomes dirt. Eyelash, teapot, insect,
Bird's claw, shoe sole, flesh—no
Matter the stages, whether buried or burned

With ceremony, or trucked to the dump—
They sift through screens, around doors, to rest
At last ionically pasted on windows.
And now while the glass is still dark
With dirt, the window delivering nothing
Of the world, only its opaque self,

She does not wish to look *through* the window
But *at* its smudgy pointillist grip
On our afterlife in particles,
Unknowable, except as faith reveals:
Smoke, grit, dust, oil
Plastered right under our noses

And pressing their claim, the inescapable
Evidence of things unseen, substance
Grimily palpable, of survival—
What we always hope, if not
Exactly *as* we hope it. Enough.
This apartment has a view, occluded

Far too long. She vows to keep
The windows clean, to look out twice
Each day—once at the traffic grid's
Kinetic fury, once at the slow-
Revolving night, the sparking and
Extinguishing of a thousand squares of light. ❋

Change Color   Marion Menna

I am seated in a black faux-leather pedicure chair, the remote
set to full body massage, my feet soaking in hot blue water. Nail
salons are big business. Did they come in with the rise of the
middle class or the feminist movement? I prefer the small shops
operated by folks from some Asian country I know I will never
visit, rather than the big deluxe spas. It feels more intimate and
yet remains impersonal. We rarely speak the same language.

Almost all the teachers at the Special Ed school had manicured
finger nails. I did not. I liked to get my hands into the paint or
clay I gave the children. And there was a little girl who screamed
in terror when a certain visitor entered our room. This someone
had very red fingernails. I tended to agree with the distraught
kid, but did not scream.

It never occurred to me to go a nail salon then. It was only
after the divorce and the move to Florida where I wore sandals
all the time that I began to think how pleasing it would be to
have shell-pink toenails. I started to frequent a salon in a nearby
shopping center where there were many young Asian women
worked. I found I liked looking at them, their graceful ways,
their careful manners. It made me think of my father and his
taste for beautiful women, the women in every man's fantasy.

Most of the technicians in this upstate New York salon,
however, are thin young men in jeans and sweaters. They are
not particularly handsome. Each looks a little like a high school
student in a chemistry lab. They chat to each other in their own
mélange of sounds and syllables, chuckling over some inside joke
I can only guess at. Perhaps the size of my feet that are bigger
than theirs.

I feel anonymous, and yet I enjoy the pressure of their hands
massaging my calf muscles and the halting way they try to sell
me sea salt scrubs for my heels, or frenching for my toenails, or

heaven forbid, waxing for my eyebrows, all of which I turn down with a smile and shake of my head, no, thank you.

Their names are John, Michael, and Lee. Easy names to remember. I do not call in advance for an appointment, content to take anyone who is available to service me. My needs are simple, really. I want my toenails cut short, the callouses filed down, and the massage to my legs, then the shell-pink nail polish. I want my fingernails filed oval and short, the cuticles trimmed, and a thin coat of clear polish applied. All the garden dirt washed away and the rough edges filed down.

Of course, I can do all this myself at home. I can still bend down and reach my toes, thanks to yoga. I can still bring one foot into my lap to work on the toenails. It is somewhat awkward doing the right hand with the left hand, but I can manage it if I really try. I enjoy the luxury, which feels like a necessity of an hour every few weeks, sitting in the throne-like massage pedicure chair. It allows me to think and remember.

One of my jobs when I was about nine years old and my mother was still alive had been to cut her toenails. Obese and ill, she could not bend over, even to put on her own shoes. Her feet were very large and wide. Her toenails were thick and woody. Ordinary toenail clippers were ineffective. It was only when my mother and I found a wood-cutting set in a local thrift shop for my brother Bob that we discovered the perfect tool — a small sharp wire clipper with very pointed tips that allowed me to get in under the woody nail and begin to clip slowly along the outer edge, careful not to go into the living flesh.

In Florida when I first began frequenting the local salon, a young woman technician squatted down and tried to put my sandals on for me. "I'll do that," I had blurted out. The girl smiled, shrugged her shoulders, and walked away. I have since learned that it is not humbling work. It is a service.

Now I sit admiring my clean, scrubbed feet. They look to me like sea creatures, or some form of plant life, unrelated to my body. Lee looks up from his stool at the base of the chair and says, "Change color?"

"No, no," I say, smiling at him. "They're perfect." ✻

A Wife for the Twenty-First Century (Newly Defined)

Raphael Kosek

I am the wife of the fork
and the spoon and the knife,
of the bowls rattling in their cupboard,
of the howling of the house.

I am the wife of the velvet muzzled dog,
the delicate cat, of the lilacs bowing
outside the window, of the moon —
sleepless white eye of the night.

I am the wife of the bad dream,
the sweating and falling, the shoe
and the slipper, of the traffic
and the rain, of church on Sunday,

and the sea in July. I am the wife
of those who let themselves go,
who reach for the bottle, the hammer,
— small angry god of war.

I am the wife of the fly and the gnat that
cluster and shine in the eye of the dead.
Of the crow that swings down
on such carrion spread. I am the wife

of intemperate grief, the river rising,
brittle limbs bending back in a wind
all trouble, all promise, all scatter.
Black cloak of the heart — you summon

me like the blackbird's high whistle
whose call becomes the thin song
of my life. I am the wife who will weep
when the eye of the world

closes, and the last flock flaps away
tearing the drop-cloth of sky that
separates this life from the other,
the husband from the wife. ❋

Days of Our Breakfast

Brittany Ambrosio

I woke up early today.
I think I'll make you breakfast.
Your favorite: scrambled eggs, bacon, and toast.
It smells good in the kitchen.
I set the table, poured your coffee,
I even flipped open the paper for you.
It's perfect.
Until I realized,
I burnt the toast.
You come down the stairs,
and after everything I've done, the coffee, the paper, the eggs
all I can think is
oh no, I burnt the toast.
I can't cover it with butter, that won't do.
You'd notice.
And I can't scrape it away because then it's nothing more than
mushy bread and burnt toast crumbs.
I have to make us new toast,
but it's going to take a while.
The toaster has to heat up
and the eggs will get cold
and the bacon will get hard
and all I can think about is
how I burnt the toast.
Oh sure, I know you've made mistakes too,
You've spilled milk before, I've seen you.
But milk can be easily cleaned up.
I made a mistake and now
I can't unburn toast. ❀

Downfall   *Sandra Sturtz Hauss*

Lady Jane visited nightly, first chatting
amiably, soon stumbling over words,
by midnight stumbling over the rest of us.
So pretty, slender, a good neighbor;
seemingly respectable, but always one cigarette,
one Screwdriver, one married lover away
from respectability.

Dear Jane, her ash blonde hair
primly pulled back, revealing the lovely
face of a fallen Irish Catholic; she
punctuated stories with props, puffed,
sipped and tittered, smoothed her hair.
Always spilling drinks, then tears, finally
secrets we should never have been privy to.

Lonely Jane, every day a liquid lunch;
suit stained, lips smeared, awaiting
the inevitable pink slip. We can only
wonder how she made her way home,
negotiated the road, the long hallways
leading to her apartment.

Finally sobered, Poor Jane,
after a late-night stumble
found in her bathtub
not in proverbial gin,
but scalding water. ❊

Waiting at the Ritz   *Jo Salas*

(Excerpt from *My Dance with Dahna*)

Tall men surround them as they leave the car, employees of his father, who owns the hotel. She looks past their burly shoulders and catches the eye of one of the photographers, who hails her as though they were old friends and snaps a volley of rapid shots before she escapes through the gleaming gilt doors of the Paris Ritz. In the elevator up to her lover's suite, he embraces her as though they were alone. The bodyguards stare at the changing numbers of the floors as though the most glamorous couple in the world is not kissing in front of them.

High above the busy boulevard, the rooms are enormous and quiet. Vases of white roses and orchids. Three bottles of champagne in a huge silver cooler. The guards leave them at the door. They are alone again. They lie down on quilted pale blue silk, but he is restless.

"I'll be back, darling. Enjoy yourself."

She manages a small smile. He seems to be intent on something, one of his ingratiating surprises, she has no idea what and doesn't care. The day is passing too slowly. Only a few hours left, and then she will go home. Home to England, to her boys. She amuses herself with the things that usually comfort her, a team of hairdressers, an expert massage. She lies still under the masseur's skillful hands. They feel kind, those hands. She is grateful, though aware that it is purchased kindness. Has anyone in her life ever shown true kindness to her?

She had thought, for a while, that her lover and his father were kind. They cradled her bruised self in their family warmth, sheltering her, comforting her, giving her a haven, at least for a while. She flowered with their attentions, feeling loved and safe.

She had never felt loved and safe in her husband's family. Never. Even at their most private it was not possible to simply relax and take pleasure in each other's casual company. There was, instead, a dense and invisible web of rules, hundreds of years of rules waiting to be shattered by the gauche foot of an outsider. They had no idea how cruel they were, how medieval. She remembered the grandmother, over one of those interminable teas during the engagement, talking in her soft, relentless voice about carrying on the monarchy, what a solemn responsibility it was, how important to be certain that one was worthy and ready. She had listened, murmuring agreement, unsure where this was leading but thrilled with the sense of history and destiny, the humbling honor of being chosen as a vessel.

Then a few days later the consultation in the rooms of the royal gynecologist. He was cordial enough, though formal. Too patrician himself to wear a white coat. He sat behind his desk in his elegant suit asking her the most personal questions about her menstruation, any diseases or infections, her mother and sisters and their reproductive history. He asked about previous boyfriends — had there been penetration? He wrote down her barely audible responses, not looking at her scarlet face. Then he told her to undress, and scrutinized and probed the contours and cavities of her body while she lay stretched out on the examining table like a cadaver in a laboratory. She'd never before been examined by a doctor whose concerns were unrelated to her own wellbeing. She had submitted, as she submitted to all of it.

He reported — she was told later — to his employers that she was magnificently ready for childbearing and yes, intact. It was only much later, years later, that she let herself hear the enraged voice within her that wanted to shriek, to the doctor, to the grandmother, to the promiscuous prince and his parents: How dare you?

Lying on the massage table she shudders.

The masseur pauses. "Are you cold, your Highness?"

"No, I'm all right. Thank you."

He continues the stroke. He doesn't know, she thinks, that they stripped me of "Her Royal Highness" a year ago, punishment for my wicked ways. I don't care what they call me. I hardly know what to call myself.

Her lover's father had his own plans. He had offered her as a trophy to his charming, clueless son to render her an instrument of revenge against those who had humiliated him, who had refused to admit him, in spite of his fabled wealth, to the table of the truly elite. Thick as a plank, she once claimed about herself, and yet she was smart enough to discern that he was rubbing his hands at the thought of a wedding and then children who would be of his blood. A devastating slap in the royal face.

His son wasn't capable of such ambition. For him she was simply the shiniest and most expensive of all his shiny and expensive acquisitions. He would love the idea of marriage and babies, of course. At least for a while. ❋

On Some Days Her Monotonous Life Was Made Confusing and Frightening by Her Thoughts

Karen Schoemer

(From Jean Rhys, *After Leaving Mr. Mackenzie*)

Mysterious open-beaked creature
on a wallpaper branch sprouting fungus
and queerly-shaped fruit,

you keep me company as the light
purples and flattens. You enlarge, distend,
until my head fits neatly inside yours.

In Paris, the darkening is loss of hope.
Night is strange here, the people beasts.
Their rumble rises like the sea.

If I could lift myself from this bed,
switch on the lamp and dress
not for evening but merely to frame myself

in a hotel window's whiskey-yellow,
I could be a chance companion to a passer-by,
hurrying beneath a lamppost's shining eye. ✳

Zelda Speaks   *Victoria Sullivan*

Scott says I'm "ill." He means "crazy," but he says
ill because that's easier to deal with, don't you see?
For him, not me. I don't really care if I'm crazy because
the stars are falling from the ebony sky, I think I'll
probably die with my boots on, and no one really loves me
anymore. Not Scott, not anyone. You have a few fits,
drool in public, and suddenly no one remembers your name,
your face. You lose your place in the great social parade.
I know I saw a marmoset, a bony thing, laughing up
her skirts at fat Gertrude's the other day. We say
we show up to talk about art, but really everyone is
fucking someone and Scott tells them all I'm ill.

I don't mind. We southern girls are great pretenders.
I've been on benders where no one got sober for eight days.
On the beaches in Antibes, we just sunned and drank
and drank and sunned. Back then my hair was golden,
and my panties stank from days of peeing in them.
Well the boys were pretty and the girls were swell,
and nobody minded if you didn't pay your bills because
back then we were the golden people. Everyone wanted
to be at the parties we attended until they didn't
and I started screaming and broke bone china.
Perhaps you've heard about this. People talk.

But that wasn't me, you see, just a female hyena
who borrowed my body for a week or two. When she was through
with me so was everyone else. Life is a party, of course,
but you have to pay the piper when the party goes sour.
Mine did. I've paid. Now I watch the flies climbing
the strange, stained walls and wonder why
the windows are barred. They are, you know.

Scott says I'll go home soon.
I've heard that story before.
No one here has any decent booze. Believe me, I've asked.

I always understood the rules of the game.
I don't place blame. We were golden.
Now is a different time. Do you like to play cards?
I never learned bridge, but I think a cocktail is a civilized
way to end the day. I like the slender stem of the martini glass.
Everything changes all the time. When I do go home,
I plan to avoid the sharp knives. They have a way of cutting
one's throat when one isn't even looking. Have you noticed that?
I never accuse Scott of drinking too much. That puts him
in a mean mood, and he's nicer when he's funny and sunny.
My Scott. I've always loved him. Do you suppose
I could go home for the weekend? Just two days.
I'd like to sleep in my own soft bed again, awake to yellow finches
and a sky of blazing sunshine on the white beach bones. ❋

Beauty, Money, Luck,
Etc for Beginners   *Anne Gorrick*

A spell
to make someone read and write like a vampire
to make someone fall in love with the color of your eyes
to make someone call you
to become a mermaid
to find a job
to become a fairy or a werewolf
to control someone
to control water and change its gender
Your future enemies will drop all charges
and draw someone into a dissolved anger
Do I dream of a future you?
Can you enhance your psychic abilities toward truth?
Erase love
Erase a broken heart
End memory
I want to find lost objects and forget about them simultaneously
A spell to fly, to grow wings and get someone to leave you alone
How can I sweeten you?
Invoke a stalking spirit and infect someone's dream
Spells to jump higher, to visit Japan or a junkyard
She wanted to look like someone else and levitate objects
Spell "tongue"
Spell "tornado"
Open a portal and overcome an enemy
Put someone to sleep on protected property, erudite
Quit smoking, quit drinking, quiet noisy neighbors
read and write someone into your life
I'd like to raise the dead and remove any bad luck, curses or obstacles
I'd like to see spirits switch bodies to stop gossip

Turn into a girl, a dragon, a vampire, a werewolf, a pig
Turn back time so we can talk to these animals
A spell to undo a spell
To unlock doors
To undo a jinx
To unblock buried belongings
I'd like to vanquish powerful demons and sell vinyl to collectors
Spell Tokyo
Spell toy
Spell crush
What are some beginner potions that really work?
A couple became shapeshifters, and became each other
The way a full moon dominates us
Change your hair color and control the elements
Harm, hurt, have, heal
Spells to make it snow love on you
Spells to avoid food
Reflect negative energy and rewind time
To unbind, to use with semen, to use with compelling oil on
mythical beasts
To crush your dreams

Acne, anxiety, bigger werewolf breasts, clear skin, confidence,
daylight, destroying demons, employment, forgiveness,
finding things that are lost, gambling and growing hair, house
protection, impotence, invisibility, jealousy, karma, keeping a
job, lucid dreams, lottery, misfortune, money luck, more beauty,
making lucky charms, new tooth, a new moon to open the
mouth, prophetic dreams, quick cash, rain, roaches, revenge,
running faster, rice, safe travel, snow, super powers, talismans,
telekinesis, to make someone move away, unwanted houseguests,
vampirism for oblivion, vehicle protection, wishes, exes, your
heart's desire, zombies

Astral projection during a waning moon
an addiction to abundance
Beauty money luck, etc for beginners
Dog dreams, incurable diseases and increased creativity
Kissing under a lunar eclipse for non-witches, an oblivion
Riding bad habits, studying sleep and using people's personal objects
Spells for vehicle registration

The stars will declare who you are ✳

PART 4

RELATIONSHIPS

Lost Gardens   *Karen Rippstein*

Words tumble from my childhood diary
abandoned like that garden
of dead red tulips, that garden
left behind with its silent fragrance
of faded petals.

In that diary thrives a bird flapping
across a pale northern sky, a garden
where a father and daughter spot
the first robin's shimmering red breast
hopping along rows of blossoming flowers.

In the nest of those words lives
another garden whose scent lingers
of cinnamon where a grandfather's
red carnations sit in a white window box
near the patio of his Florida home,
where three generations gather
lacey red blooms for the dinner table
each Sunday.

In that child's diary between pages,
the far off fragrance of gardens are found,
the gardens that held us all,
father and daughter, grandfather and
granddaughter.

In this garden, I trace a robin's *cheerup,*
cheerily, cheerup arriving at its nest above
the red granite *Pace* headstone and place
a vase of fresh cut flowers between two graves. ✳

Red Flowers   *Dinah Dietrich*

Mother planted bright red flowers
in her garden —
Hummingbirds came,
their bright wings
beating fast, a blur
of wings — hovering

Mother told me
how she gave birth
how she watched in a mirror
until pain produced me finally
pushing me out
from that dark place
between her thighs ✳

My Mother Wants Lambchops, Steaks, Lobster, Roast Beef

Lyn Lifshin

something to get
her teeth in.
Forget the shakes
cancer patients
are supposed to
choose, forget
tapioca pudding,
vanilla ice,
she wants what
is full of blood,
something to
chew to get
the red color
out of, something
she can attack
fiercely. My
mother, who never
was namby pamby,
never held her
tongue, never
didn't attack
or answer back,
worry about
angering or hurt-
ing anybody but
said what she
felt and wouldn't
walk any tight
rope, refuses the
pale and delicate

for what's blood,
what she can
chew, even spit
out if she
needs
to ※

Back to School

Kate Hymes

Lock the door; don't let anyone in!
Momma left right after breakfast,
left us alone to care for ourselves.
She came back in the afternoon
arms loaded with bags and boxes.

On the four poster spread with pink,
she laid out the treasures:
pink and blue flowered cotton
panties and undershirts,
crisp, swishy petticoats,
red and blue plaid
gathered skirts, pleated skirts,
jumpers with white blouses,
full-skirted dresses with Peter Pan collars.
Brand new for back to school.

We never chose a dress or shoe
from a store's racks and stacks.

We never heard the words:
You can't try that on here.
Use the colored dressing room.

We never stood in line waiting
while the salesclerk served
tow-headed children and their Mommas
first. We didn't see the pickets
parading *Freedom Now* signs
in front of Woolworth's, didn't see
the passers-by shove and push and
spit and yell *Nigger!*

We waited at home excited
for Momma all flushed and breathless,
carrying her downtown load.
We waited at home anxious
fingers crossed that what she chose
was what we wanted. ✤

Navigating with Mother   *Laura Jan Shore*

The Hudson River runs through your drowsy afternoons,
static, crackling like tumbled stones.

You flew a sea plane solo, the length of these currents as a girl,
swam in it, skated on it, and painted this landscape with oils.

Now you stare past tangled banks of unplucked berries
to the shrouded depths
contained by granite palisades.

Renouncing claim to your frail bones and muddied brain,
you've seeped out somehow —
evaporated into the miasma.

And you want to know, *How shall I cross the river?*

Mornings find you adrift as you stir your coffee,
white billows cresting the waves.

Beneath the swirls, a strange light
flirts with you, something lost, fluttering
before it sinks out of sight.

Surfing the crosscurrents of your moods
where river turns estuary, where saltwater meets sweet,

black-beaked swans surface
fierce in the face of your grief.

Clutching your walker,
like a drowning woman in a swollen river —
waters surge to the sea.

Even when your eyelids droop shut,
you are watching its copper back
snake towards the city.

Then wake to ask, *How shall I cross?*
And who? Who's going with me? ❋

My Father and the Floating House: At an Exhibit of Chagall's Paintings at the Thyssen Bornamisza Museum

Jan Zlotnik Schmidt

In the museum in Madrid, I think of you. Not a likely place.
You knew no Spanish; you hated your trip to Spain. The late
night dinner hours. The brooding darkness and melodrama of
the culture. The bull fights. Not even the lapping waters, thin
streams and fountains of the Alhambra caught your fancy.

But now here in Madrid you come back to me. A voiceless
presence. I stare at the Chagall paintings. The liquid blue skies,
white floating carnations like confetti, the fiddler perched on a
roof with a violin bow arched against his chin and the cosmos.
The primary colors swirl around me. In a vortex with floating
cows, red goats and steers, roosters, and grooms, red poppies, and
the bride with her transparent veil—all swimming around me.

You were never in this Russia. Never in this world of
memory, longing, loss or myth. Zlotnik. A gold coin. A place
near a gold mine. Slotnicki (in Czech) a jeweler. The name is
all you had. And the thick guttural heaves and savage "ss" of
Russian — Strazvodya, spasiba, dosvedanya. Or those aching
Yiddish vowels and consonants that led to your mother's kitchen,
to boiled yellow chicken, borscht and shav. In my visits to her
house, the carp and white fish, still alive, swam in the bath tub.
The potatoes with bulbous eyes lived in the underwear drawer,
popping out of her gatkes. The yellow onions were caught in her
voluminous bras and flowered housedresses. In her dementia, the
bedroom became her pantry, and in time the tine of a fork went
against the neck of the caretaker who tried to stop her ranting.
You shut your eyes to this and put her away.

No large green eye in a red house. No Persian blues or
cardinals red. Just the stolid father who looked like Krushchev

and banged his words against your bowed head. And instead you became a man who loved English words, sonnets, Shakespeare, Latinate syllables. Greek myths. The Iliad. The Odyssey. No voyages down the Volga. Now, in old age, in senility, all words have left you. You live in shadows, in a mysterious gray silence I cannot penetrate.

I go back to a shetl, to houses of sticks and mud. To browned fields of grain. To small dusty purple plums that I bought from an old woman in black who sold them on the side of the road on the way to Krakov. Did you ever go back to that deserted history? That history that brought nothing, no poetry, no words to your lips? Once I asked you if your father talked about his past in the Ukraine. Without much emotion or thought, you said plainly no. You knew little about him before he became your father.

The colors and figures skitter around me. The blue jester lies against the neck of a huge white rooster, a red steer jumps into the sky, a grass green village tilts against green mountains, a cobalt blue house drifts through space, a young girl pushes a white horse's rump, a red house holds a yellow candle burning in its midst. There are winged, floating angels, brides, and grooms, and bouquets of anemones. And always the shetl floating in the background and sometimes a red goat fiddler.

I eye this world. See your shuttered eyes. Your poet's consciousness gone. Was your world always in sepia tones? Were you weighted down by the prospect of that darkened world? And bearing that weight, did you choose to shed it, like a heavy cloak? Leaving you no warmth, no past, no color. ✳

My Father, 1928   *Mary Makofske*

When you rose in morning dark,
strapped your feet in thick-soled boots
to stumble down the walk, down streets
where men and women lolled,
tangled in blankets, dreams, and arms
of those they loved, and did not love,
when you turned in the open gate,
the yard where horses waited
for your touch, horses whose names
you never forgot—Samson, Abel,
Seth, and Job—what did you want?

Where did you go as you followed
a horse's balloon of breath, the echo
of his iron-clad step, down streets
whitewashed with winter, chiming
milky bottles against stoops and peering
in steamy windows of flats and houses?

The empties rattled like the change
you couldn't keep in your pocket.
Someone had given you the route
and a horse that knew it. You let
the reins go slack in your hands. ❀

How to Put a Fish to Bed   *Rebecca Schumejda*

> *"Fish," he said softly, aloud,*
> *"I'll stay with you until I am dead."*
> —ERNEST HEMINGWAY

I have been reading *The Old Man and The Sea*
to my four-year-old daughter until she falls asleep,
averaging three to four pages each night.
For weeks now, we've been in the skiff
with Santiago struggling with the marlin,
holding the line for him when he gets too weary.
Each night, her last words dangle helplessly in the air
like everything else we haven't gotten around to yet:
When are we going to catch the fish?

During our days, my husband and I struggle
to keep our cars running, our bills paid,
and food on the table. I have been questioning if
there really is honor in struggle, defeat, then death
until tonight when finally he harpoons the marlin
through the heart. I look over at her and she asks
what we are going to do now, but before I have a
worthy answer, a cloud of blood disperses into
shark infested waters and she drifts toward dreams. ❧

Blue Baby

Colleen Geraghty

(From *My Mother's Icons*)

Even if Vincent *was* born a blue baby, he was one of the lucky ones. On account of all Grandmom's cooking and her massaging his joints with every kinda grease she kept in the stove can, Vincent lived a heck of a long time. We found out about Vincent accidentally by accident on account of our own blue baby. Baby Joey was born blue, not the blue of sky blue, gotta-love-it Easter egg blue but the kinda purpled-up blue a woman's got the Sunday after her man's had way too much tying it up good with the boys after his Saturday job and he goes over to throw' em back. Comes home raring to go with a head so big it can't fit through the door.

Baby Joey was the Sunday after a Saturday, meat-on-your eye kinda blue. At least that's what Mary-T said that Aunt Nora said that Mrs. Larkin said when she was folding diapers.

"I seen that baby of Maura's yesterday. Holy Mary have mercy on us, he's a blue baby if I ever saw one. Got a hole right up in his heart."

Mary-T said it kinda brag-like, which set my sister to crying so hard and my big sister wasn't a spiller, not like the rest of us crying brats, so I knew that Baby Joey musta had it bad.

Never heard before of a blue baby, but sure enough that Joey had come home, all small and tucked up in on himself and fragile like a baby chick hatched out of an egg — wrinkled up and rattling — and my Mom was so quiet with him. She hardly gave my baby sister a look and her crying in her crib or her playpen — fit to be tied. Her bottle woman, my Mom, home but her just saying: "Get your sister." "Feed your sister." "Change your sister." "Rock your sister." "Bathe your sister." "Shut your sister up, Joey's sleeping." And my baby sister not getting it that she wasn't no baby no more. Her just crying in her crib, fit to be tied.

"She better get to crawling soon or holding up her own bottle cause I'm sure sick of this shit," I said. And my big sister set to pummeling me like I was a boxing bag.

"You shut up, you hear me, shut up!" Her holding my other baby brother who was wobbling now all over the house and lifting himself up all over things so much that we had to keep him in a second playpen.

What a mess a blue baby can make. Baby Joey wasn't normal. My Dad had said it, and so we had to be extra good. My sister carrying my wobbly brother around on her hip and me carrying my baby sister around, praying she'd get her fingers on straight soon cause she was one ugly bitch baby wanting my Mom's lap. I nearly drowned her trying to shove that bottle nipple down her throat.

"Get your sister." "Rock your sister." "Feed your sister." "Shut your sister up." And all the while, us eating cold sandwiches while my Mom cooed it up good to Baby Joey and his scrawny blue self. Don't get me wrong and stuff, I coulda liked Joey and probably kinda loved him, but he was hard to know on account of him being kept like a fragile little bird up in my mom's bedroom, and her sitting, sitting, and sitting with him, waiting for him to get big enough for the doctors to cut him up good and fill up that hole that was blowing windy through his little chicken heart.

But like I said before, Vincent was the only blue baby we ever heard of to live long enough to stand up in a bathtub for hair-washing time, and my Aunt Nora said that's what killed him in the end. "A shower can sure be a deadly thing," she said, "especially if you're born blue."

It sort of shocks you, I guess, and Vincent got it good that day, turning blue beyond his lips and quivering up like burned paper. Grandmom grabbing him and running crazy out into the yard.

"Jesus, Mary and Joseph, that's bloody awful!" Mary Rafferty said, "Dead from a shower, that's hideous."

Like I said, we found out about Vincent, my Dad's ghost brother, who no one ever mentioned and nobody ever saw, not even a picture on Grandmom's picture shelf. We found out about Vincent being the longest living blue baby when my mom's blue Baby Joey just shriveled up and died in his bassinet one Sunday morning before Mass. My mom was taking a shower and Baby Joey must a heard that water running while Vincent blew windy words into his heart hole — telling Baby Joey all about his own shower shock and Baby Joey just shit himself, shriveled up, and died.

Mary-T said, "Vincent came for Baby Joey cause shower shocking a blue baby's hard enough without being dead and lonely without another blue friend to keep you company."

"At least he ain't lonely anymore," my sister said and then she got to crying so hard, I had to hit her. ❈

When Granny Made My Lunch

Bobbi Katz

I always dreaded those days—
those embarrassing days—
when Granny made my lunch.
Her signature, a bulging brown paper bag,
dotted with grease stains—
bullying in front of the breakfast milk
so there was no way I could avoid
taking it out.
No way it could possibly be "forgotten".

In the quiet of the kitchen,
I could imagine the brown bag
broadcasting itself
with the pungent smell of raw onion
and rendered chicken fat
in the room where we hung our coats
and shelved our lunches.
I could hear the wild rumpus of smells—
fortissimo by noon.

At Mt. St. Mary's
the day students ate in the gym,
edging the basketball court in dark green jumpers
pulled over brown stockinged calves,
eyeing each other's lunches,
ready to swap half an egg salad
for half a bologna.
How I envied those neat flat rectangles
on packaged white bread.
Predictable.
Perfect.
Granny's sandwiches were left whole.

She wasn't taking any chances
that I might make a bad deal
for peanut butter and jelly
from a stranger's house.

On Granny days I tried
to hide my sandwich
but how could I?
Exotic.
Gigantic.
A brass band of a sandwich
clamoring for attention!
The chopped liver heaped
between uneven slabs of pumpernickel
or sliced brisket piled on ragged rye.
And always,
always
the raw onion —
a Jewish star
in this place of crosses
marking me as an outsider.

No matter that Granny gave me an apple
and an orange.
No matter that she gave me a love token —
a napkin tied with a snip of ribbon —
a purse full of almonds and raisins.
The raw onion betrayed me.
It made me different
from the girls at Mt. St. Mary's
and sister to those girls —
those other girls —
girls I only knew from pictures —
foreign girls from Poland and Rumania —

their faces pale and frightened
and a Jewish star
sewn on their coats. ❋

Birthmark

Joann K. Deiudicibus

We talk of cleaning the rugs, under
the rugs, and suddenly
I enter into another childhood

like the cat I dropped off in the town
where I was born
one hour from home.

I have found my way here.
I know the face of the strange woman
who gave birth to me in St. Anthony's.

I don't know this blue house
but remember our eyes, their right angles,
each a tidy room with torn-screen centers:
and her dyed blonde hair
curling tightly like a daughter's fist
about her mother's finger. ※

Geechee Daughter –
for Fahja & Zachary

Brenda Connor-Bey

It was a shadow passing
Brief yet slow enough for her to feel
Like breaths of seaweed
Whispering in her ear

But she turned away

She's always heard them
greetings from the sea
Laughter and wisdomwords from the lady
And the man, whose footprints touched the earth
Long and narrow like hers
The crooked smile she wears as her own

But she shuts herself off now
Turns her head
Closes her eyes and ears

Old rituals in a new day
She summons without drums
Without candles
Without chants
Closed eyes, deep breaths, a shudder
And they were there

That was up north
Where shoes removed at the front door
filth of street and thoughts left outside
a life where sweeping was done in daytime only

Now hands touch the soft rise of her belly
Feels her son dancing to music he knows
Gullah songs deep within

Ocean air, mud, shrimp, crab
Whisper his biblical name
And the shadow shifts abruptly
Pulling her into the sun

Eat crackers, chile
Yo mouf won't fill up
Wit so much water

A high c-note splashes
Through receding tides
Beyond breakers and boats
Sees a woman holding his hand
Laughing ✳

Wednesdays with Miss Wolfstein *Gretchen Primack*

I should have been more devoted.
Loved the round black notes, the swirl
of treble clef. Her knuckles, big as drawer pulls,
knocked the iron stand in three-four time;

Johann Strauss waltzed her around
the piano bench through clouds
of rosin, a curtain of horsehair,
leaned her across the keys.

Tonight, black-wrapped bodies
and polished wood make music,
whorled sounds, electric green reeds
in a silver bowl. The soloist

has worn her chin to callus
for the chance to be what is sad and rich
and endless, what can be lost,

and the loss. Miss Wolfstein bends
to scratch a note above the third measure.
Her body hums. She is always
inside it. It is always inside her. ❋

A Reminiscence Based on Photos
Found in Different Places
in Deference to James Agee
and Walker Evans   *Mary Fakler*

A rummage and storage company has been hired to clean out the
old homestead of Clara and Ulysses Mumble. They begin in the
attic—an old picnic basket, its straw sides broken and ripped,
filled with old photos. The artifacts of lives once lived.

There's Charlie Graham and the boys; it might be the day the
Lyceum team took the pennant. There's the kids at Playland, the
midday sun reflecting off the boardwalk into their smiling faces.
Mama and her sisters beside the old oak on the front lawn; their
hats sit perkily atop their bobbed hairdos.

And there's Mama Clara and Pop Pop, the matriarch and patriarch
of the clan—on their wedding day. June 11, 1942, just before Pop
Pop went off to England to drop bombs on the enemy. Sacred Heart
Church in Yonkers. Somehow, I remember that day, even though it
was long before I came on the scene, before my own Mama, even.

Uncle Tommy's boots are up there, too. They said he had them
on when they went into the Argonne. Those boots and his dog
tags were the only things Mama Clara had left of her oldest boy.
Lucy Ann and I used to put them on and trudge around the attic
in them when we were kids. But one time, Mama Clara came
upstairs and caught us. She was so angry she almost whipped us.
She took them, then, and we never knew where she had put them.

The old house is going on the auction block in a week or two.
No one wants to pay good money for a big old three-storied
Victorian which sits like a lonely watchman beside a defunct
railroad track. Even though no trains can be seen or heard
anymore, the sight of the tracks turns people away.

My Dad always said the house was in the perfect shape and the
perfect location to be a brothel.

Pop Pop and his lifelong friend, Johnny James, used to sit
out on the front porch drinking iced tea and arguing about the
fate of the world and all that's wrong with it. They grumbled
about people who complain about America. Both had served
in the armed forces; both were fiercely patriotic and loyal. I
remember Johnny James telling Pop Pop he was going to make
a sign that said, "If you don't like our country, move out!" The
American flag was a permanent fixture in the front window for
as long as I can remember.

Pop Pop always sat opposite Johnny James, in the rocker he
had inherited from old Uncle Rufus. It seems that he moved
constantly—back and forth, back and forth. We could hear the
squeak of the wood-on-wood all the way up on the third floor.
The tempo of the entire house seemed to adhere to it. When the
train roared by, before it slowed down and stopped in Ellotsville,
instead of stopping their talk, Pop Pop and Johnny James
would yell over the noise. Their voices bouncing off the sides
of the speeding train hit the discolored walls of the house and
reverberated all around it. ❋

Learning to Read   *Rachel Elliott Rigolino*

He lies down on the grass, gazing up into the cloudless sky, closing his eyes to find those red-gold memories of walking to school in the fall with his friends. He loved getting out of the house. Most mornings, he found his mother slumped at the end of the couch, huddled under the blue-and-white crocheted blanket made by a great-aunt no longer remembered. On those rare occasions when the house was quiet, he would discover her perched on the edge of a cushion, gazing out the smeared plate glass window at the morning. But she never went outside.

At school, Mrs. Gumble taught him to count, color, and read. She bent over him, telling him to sound out the words. "H-h-h-h. That's the letter 'h', Gillie." Gillie, what a shitty name for a boy, but the way Mrs. Gumble said it, the "G" came out harder, tougher than when his mother slurred it. "Jillie, will ya run to the store and get me a Snickers bar, honey?"

"H-h-hop." That's it. "H-h-op on p-pop." Good, Gillie. Her eyes were not moist and runny like his mothers. They were clear. Brown, he thinks or maybe hazel. How old was Mrs. Gumble, he wonders now. Maybe 30 or 40, she had brown hair that she wore in a straight cut to her chin. It was soft because he had touched it one day.

"Why Gillie, do you like my hair?" She seemed only a little bit surprised. Surprised in a calm, good way, not like when he came home and found his father sitting on the stoop with a can of Miller. "What the fuck you looking at?"

"H-h-op on P-pop." The little bears or whatever were jumping on their father's stomach. "St-st-op. Do not h-hop on p-p-op!"

"Gillie, how wonderful! You sounded that sentence out all by yourself." He remembered, noticing the little mustache on Mrs. Gumble's face, and then feeling guilty because she always made him feel so good.

"Stop it! Stop it!" He was screaming, screaming so loudly that his father paused momentarily to look up and away from the blue-and-white mound he had been pounding with his fist. A smile crossed his father's face, "You want a piece of it? Huh?" Standing erect, he shuffled towards him.

"Mr. B-broon." He stopped, something wasn't right. "Try again, Gillie. Go ahead." "Mister Brown, Mr. Brown is out of town."

"Good boy, Gillie." She put her hand over his. "Gillie, is everything all right?" He didn't expect her question. He nodded and stared her right in the eye. For Mrs. Gumble, he was always going to be all right.

He remembered the last time he saw Mrs. Gumble. Maybe he was in sixth or seventh grade. He was in the market buying something for his mother. "Gillie, is that you? I can't believe how big you are."

"Not much," was what he had said when she asked him whether he still read books. But she didn't seem at all disappointed. She just smiled. "I'm sure you are going to do very well in high school, Gillie. You're so smart and such a good reader."

The sun is beginning to burn his eyelids. He sits up and becomes a little dizzy.

"Hey Gillie, time to go inside, man." A guard is standing over him.

"Yeah, OK." Not such hard time as it turned out, not as hard as his mother had worried about. "Jillie, don't get in no more trouble, huh, promise me? Stay away from the bad ones." He had to suck his teeth at that one. Bad ones? No one else he met had stabbed his own father "repeatedly, over and over, more than forty times" as the DA had put it. No one else in here had "nearly severed the neck of a helpless man who had been confined to a wheelchair for the past two years, defenseless to the blows of his only son."

Brushing the grass from the back of his pants, he walks slowly towards the low, gray building in front of him, trying to remember only those red-gold days of October. ✳

On the Nature of Desire

Donna Spector

I told a wise man once how much I love
the earth. How I lay face down, my hands
digging through tall grasses as though,

if I held on tightly to this world
spinning its slow dance through our universe
I could stay here forever, embracing

each precarious moment. *Yes*, he said,
and this will lead to suffering. And I, being young,
replied, *Pain is just the dark side of joy.*

Older now, I think of non-desires, letting
go of wet leaves outside my window,
my snoring cats, strong coffee, chocolate,

plays, poems, dawn lighting my study window,
dusk settling over the marsh
across my road, piano sonatas, solo violins,

silly jokes, my friends and former lovers,
memories worn thin as film played endlessly—
and just writing this tells me I can't

relinquish anything. But in the midst of all
I want and love, I can descend to an inner
room. Dark here till I light a candle

that glows over bare boards and walls.
I wait: silence, though still I hear
the pulsing world outside.

This is a place of non-desire, I know,
but how can it be when I want
now to be nowhere else? ❋

The Fifty-Pound Canary   *Betty Ann Enos neé Damms*

It was in the dollar store, tucked behind other cheap toys. She
slowly reached for the small Tweety Bird, clutched it and stared
at it. It was "Made in China," so it wasn't a perfect replica of
Tweety; but it didn't matter. It was a canary, albeit a plastic
cartoon-character canary. She shifted the bottle of shampoo, the
package of writing tablets, and the scrub brush, to make room in
her hands for this absolutely necessary purchase and, forgetting
the other things on her list, hurried to the register. Silently, she
paid for the items and watched as Tweety was tucked inside the
bag. She didn't see the cashier smile, didn't hear her thanks and,
as it was, wouldn't have been able to return the smile.

Ignoring the wind that almost yanked the door out of her hand,
she hurried toward the car and, once inside, dug out Tweety and
carefully unwrapped her. After gently running her finger over the
silly bird's face, she held it to her chest and closed her eyes, then
set it on the dashboard and stared at it. Melissa would love it.

Six months ago her seven-year-old bundle of cheer, had come
home from school, dropped her backpack and called, "Mom,
Mom." After their customary hug and kiss, she'd asked, "what
did the fifty-pound canary say to the cat?"

"I have no idea. What did it say?"

In the deepest, most serious voice she could muster, Melissa
had said, "Here, kitty, kitty." They had laughed and laughed,
imagining a huge canary saying that to their big, fearless cat. And
when he'd ignore them, as cats often do, they'd say, "Here, kitty,
kitty," and dissolve into laughter.

There had always been laughter with their gregarious, funny
child, who enjoyed making people laugh. Then she got sick, and
in spite of it, she told jokes to the other children in the ward, and
as she got sicker, joked how this disease took her breath away, and
even made jokes about "the place" she was going.

She started the car and mechanically steered, directed through habit to "the place" where Melissa now rested; she stopped the car and stared at the plot, still dressed in fresh dirt. She had removed the dead flowers last week, but ribbons attached to the small shrub she'd planted waved in the breeze. Slowly, very slowly, she got out of the car and, with trembling hands, picked up Tweety and carried her to Melissa's resting spot. She gently laid it on the dirt, then decided to set it in the shrub, and tied it to a branch so it wouldn't get blown away. Finally satisfied, she stood and said in a deep voice, "Here, kitty, kitty."

For three weeks she had been devoid of emotion, and she had felt as dead as her daughter who lay in the ground, and she had known if things didn't change, her marriage would be dead, too. The tears that filled her eyes ran over, and she allowed them to run down her cheeks, fell to her knees, and sobbed. The tears became like rain that washed away her anguish. Finally spent, she rose, and with a spring in her step that hadn't been there since Melissa died, turned to the car. She dug in her purse for her cell phone, finally found it at the bottom, turned it on, and pressed the speed-dial.

"Hello," said the familiar male voice.

"Honey?" she said in her old, normal voice. "I'm coming home." ✳

The Clay Goose

Anne Richey

These forty-nine years on shelf or sill,
afloat on its blue-green base, safe —
safe-guarded through every migration

cushioned in my travel trunk or padded
in its own small box, *fragile* inked
across the top: fragile the goose,

fragile the troubled boy who made it.
Holding it, my fingers try to channel his,
shaping, smoothing, try to summon —

did he feel it? — the needful pleasure
of his power. They pause to explore
where he paused and pressed too hard,

the clay understanding. I love the rust
and creamy browns with hints of melting
yellow, the blue-green splashes on neck

and tail, the wet-shine of the glaze.
How high did the boy fly incising the V
of the back feathers' overlay, or tilting

the head in this quizzical life-like way?
Etched in the raw clay bottom, N.D.
for North Durham (the bullying ground),

N.W., my brother's initials, and 1963.
Was the torment on-going then?
The depression on the neck is a worry.

Imprint from a real time of a real boy,
now a man who's north today and south
tomorrow, like a bird trifled with

by wind or out of sync with seasons.
Rubbing the spot, if I'm not trying to
comfort the boy (a wistful exercise)

or musing on one of possible whys,
I'm reverting to my long-lost faith
in magic: rub enough, child,

your brother will come home. ❋

Modern Love: Till Death Do Us Part   *Eva Tenuto*

On June 24th, 2011, same-sex marriage became legal in New York State. With a history of openly dating men and secretly dating women, for the first time ever, at 38 years old, I was enjoying a same-sex relationship publicly. I wanted to celebrate coming out with all of New York State so when my partner, Julie, asked me to marry her, I said yes.

Our engagement was also a welcome distraction from something painful in my life: a month earlier, my 94-year-old Grandmother was diagnosed with stomach cancer.

Granny and I were always close, and as I got older, I felt I could confide in her. But, for some reason, I was scared to tell her I was involved with Julie.

"Granny," I finally announced, "I'm seeing a woman."

She sat quietly for a moment, with a strange look on her face. Oh, no, was she having a heart attack? After a pregnant pause, she asked brusquely, "Does she drink?"

"Uh, no," I said, trembling.

"Well, that's good!" she responded. End of story.

Granny knew first hand the devastation alcoholism from her marriage to my Grandfather, and was so proud that I'd broken the cycle. She came to my recovery celebrations every year. Once she was assured Julie wasn't a drunken lesbian, she welcomed her into our family with open arms. Maybe she'd even be open to the idea of us marrying some day.

By August, Granny took a turn for the worse and then rapidly continued in that direction. "I think today is the day," my mother said when she called, one afternoon.

I rushed over. I found Granny staring ahead into a place only she could see, presumably into the afterlife. I said goodbye to her when I went to bed that night.

The next day, at 7 a.m., I peeked into her bedroom prepared to find her still and breathless. Then she whipped her head around and snapped in my direction, "No one got me breakfast yet! I want oatmeal!" she demanded. I made her oatmeal. She insisted it wasn't oatmeal and that I was a liar.

It went on like this for weeks. One day she'd appear to be on the mend, and the next, was completely comatose. Hospice warned us that this was common, and it could still have been months before she passed. I should have been relieved that she was still with us, but all I felt was out of control. I wondered if I'd ever know which "goodbye" or "I love you" would be the last. I felt as if I was going to have a nervous breakdown.

Good thing I had my big gay wedding distraction. When I wasn't caring for Granny, I kept myself busy Googling women's white tuxes, bridesmaids' dresses, venues, rings and caterers. I latched onto planning my wedding, which rivaled the emotional rollercoaster of watching Granny slowly and painfully exit this world.

After a few weeks, I took a suggestion from hospice. "We are all going to be just fine, Granny," I told her. "It's okay if you're ready to go." To which she replied, "Where the hell do you think I am going? I can't get out of bed!"

At my overnight with Granny, I gathered the courage to tell her about the wedding while she was in a coherent state. With tears in her eyes, she squeezed my hand and said, "Will I be able to go?" Knowing she would surely be gone by November dampened my excitement. "No matter what," I told her, "I am sure you will be there."

The next morning I went back home after a sleepless night of waking up to help Granny. When I got home, Julie's neck was bright red and blotchy – a sure sign she'd been obsessively thinking.

"I can't do it!" she blurted. "It's not sitting right with me. I don't think we should be planning our wedding right now with all that is going on. I'm sorry, honey."

Even though a short while later I would realize that what my girlfriend did was loving—at the time, all it did was land me back into a world where my Granny, a woman who'd loved me for all 38 years of my life, was leaving me. Julie was cutting off the lifeline to my distraction, and I was furious.

"Well, if you ever ask me to marry you again," I threatened, "make sure you mean it."

On September, 20, 2011, Granny passed away. I'd convinced myself that all I would feel when Granny passed was relief, that I'd be ready to let go. But I was wrong. Nothing could prepare me for the loss that accompanied her passing, the shift in the feeling of being here on Planet Earth without her.

In the end, I was so glad my girlfriend loved me enough to do what she knew was right in her heart. Without the wedding planning distracting me, I got to be there with the one woman who mattered at that moment—Granny. I got to be by her side, fully, until the last minute, until the last breath. Until death do us part.

On December 20, 2013, after enough time had passed, Julie asked me again and, of course, I said yes! ✳

Sahara Affair   *Allison B. Friedman*

It was a good deal easier when I reviled you. I can't remember
that so much now, since you have crossed the vast desert of my
heart yet again, that barren wasteland born of decades of unmet
desires. You caught me off guard this time when you appeared
by smart phone, your number blocked, your face a billion sandy
pixels, a digital mirage. I felt woozy from the sudden heat of you.
By the time you arrived in real time, blazing for me beneath a
Saharan sun, I was already feeling wavy. You set me spinning like
a child's toy top: fast and faster still, until all my stripes blend
blue and I approach lift-off.

It is always like that with you and me. I am forever at tilt
where you are concerned, and it is safe to say that you know just
how to play me.

A desert heart is strange and mysterious, the glassy sands of
feelings and memories rearranging themselves, over and again, at
the slightest hint of a desert breeze. You traverse this sandscape
without pausing to consider the thirsts that will ensue. This
time, the voyage was long, but you pressed on, magnificently,
sandbank-by-sandbank, in urgent need of something you believe
that only I can provide. When you found me, as you always do,
I was dipping deep into an oasis of Margaritas, top shelf, three
tequilas required to anaesthetize me against the illusion I knew
we were about to create. Your ancient powers are impressive
where I am concerned. You appeared, and in that scorching
moment I forgot, as I am want to do, the many nights I have spent
filling that same desert pool with the briny tears of a woman
febrile with longing.

We set up a tent of soft Egyptian cotton with an obscene thread
count, a billowing tent for two the color of an inky night sky. We
drank the Moscato you know I like, straight from the canteen that
is its bottle. We imagined ourselves nomads braced against the

shifting sands, and we pretended it meant nothing, and that time had stopped, and that it was meaningful and necessary, and that if no one bore witness, it had not really happened.

The reviling is really much simpler, you know. It is not hard to conduct a symphony of anger inside your soul, and turn it up so loud that you hear nothing but the sound of your own heart begging you to stop. I ruined your life, you said, by reminding you of the true connection that lives beyond the boundaries of lust and desire and the conventions of commitment. Bullshit, I said, there is nothing lofty about this. You take what you want, my charming conqueror, and you always have. Do you think I haven't noticed that you cc yourself on every email you send me? Calculated, I said. I will always love you, you said. Always.

It is easy to revile a man like that: a premeditated man who believes he can outwit me with no effort at all. You plead not guilty where I am concerned, every time, and you argue your case in the interest of winning, not justice. And even sunblind and Margarita-hazy, I can see clearly that this does not resemble love. I am a temporary tattoo upon your heart, but you have marked mine indelibly, row after row of hatch marks drawn in permanent marker.

So you have returned once more, shimmering in the heat, to send me into the stratosphere above the infinite desert sky. You came and pillaged me. When you left a sudden sandstorm erupted in your wake, obscuring your departure and leaving me gasping, my silt-filled lungs unable to find my breath. You left me here, tangled in the gritty bedclothes, wondering what the hell just happened and how long it will take me to recover this time.

There is no regret, you know, quite like the regret of I-did-it-again.

Now you will disappear once more, indefinitely, into the thorny wilds. You will hide for a time in the damp and murky underbelly of a city I have always hated, leaving me to wonder what terrible desert wind erupted and carried all reason and judgment away. But before you left you ran me a hot shower just the way you know I like it. I rinsed you away, baptized myself clean. You left no trace but for a vague and arid memory, the memory of that reviling, for me to resurrect once more.

The desert is a wasteland, but I suppose you will find me there when you return. ❀

To the Unnamed One...   *Lorna Tychostup*

It was different when I didn't know you
    back before you left your Muslim god at my door.

The dark color of your eyes
pressured and lost of all control
hanging over me

the simple feel of your left foot in my right hand

the hair on your calf warm and curled under my touch

your finger making spirals in my palm . . .

A trust never trusted before
    two sixteen-year-old virgins
swarming the confines of our middle-aged hive.

Words never heard before—
    fresh seeds planted by years of loss
your hand placing mine on your heart
assuring me no distance would keep us apart.

I knew then you were telling no lies.

As the bombs fell on Fallujah
    gentle snowflakes illuminating a moonlit winter's sky
I wondered if I would ever see you again
even if you were to survive.

Would the holes left by mortars
be too far a divide
for our love to cross?

Would the visions forced on you
    so many wolves tearing apart flesh of first kill
keep your heart from opening
to mine?

It is better to think these things
than to think of you lying dead
on the side of the road
the fatigue of battle overturning you to your god

and if that wasn't enough
there were those screams coming from Abu Ghraib
forced nakedness covering unspeakable acts
Americans recreating their worst fears
inflicting on others a roiled hidden homosexuality
bared women's breasts mocked and fondled
photos of men covering themselves
raw fumblings to protect against the rabid dog's teeth

and then Seymour told of the torn screams of young boys

there are no words to make this better ...

And does the memoried image of our nakedness bring you shame?
Can you separate our mingled flesh from that brutalized by freedom?
Will this brutality speak more to our separation than to our coupling?

And in this silence I wander guided by our love ...
you said you would be with me as I slept
you said you would be with me each morning
you said you would be with me in all the hours of every day.

I wonder where you are now
and why your silence is so deafening

your
    fear
was the last thing
        I thought would keep us
            apart. ❋

The Arm

Iris Litt

I was going to get up early
and make a Things To Do list
when your sleepy arm landed
around my waist, your hand in my hand.
The digital clock said 5:30 AM, your arm
went first on top of the covers, I picked it up
and put it undercover for two good reasons,
your arm would be cold in the country dawn
but the real reason was simple,
your skin against mine in sleep. That's all:
your bare arm around my bare waist.
And outside our window, the cry of the crow.
the lighting of the sky. the sound
of the stream rolling down the mountain.
We are bears in our cave, we are deer
warming ourselves on each other.
We are part of a picture, pieces in a puzzle,
notes in a rhythm. We turn, the earth turns,
we sigh and sleep. ✻

The Burial—Sarah
(from "Union")

Jacqueline Renee Ahl

VI.
After the first night,
I put a knife to the rope of my hair,
severing its flesh from my body.
Coiled it in an old blanket, brought to the yard
like a dead baby.
Balancing shovel, lantern, bundle.
Girlhood gone.
You watched from the window while I knelt, back burning.
Down into the earth the curled years
falling away in expectation of age, dropped limbs,
something sweet and stronger.
The lamp ran low, my awkward prayer abandoned.
Dusting earth from knees and shouldering the shovel.
Door creaking.
From you, the strange embrace —
touching the shorn locks, my naked neck,
as if burned,
quizzical and silent.
Severance pay.
Nights after, you still reached up to touch
as if the ghost of her and it remained.
Less of me to pull to you, to keep.

The ground outside is alive with whispers
names groaned into her hair by men
now trapped in darkness.
She kept but one.
A single strand, bright as a wedding band,
binds her to him, in a wooden box near the bedstead.
It is just enough love. ❊

Tom's Funeral   *Cheryl A. Rice*

I have never known someone to
assert themselves as little in the coffin
as your father today.
Shadow of his former selves,
if it had not been for your
mother's cascade of recognition
I would not have known him at all,
despite seed catalogs, chocolate bars,
lap blanket the coroner threw upside down
over his bottom half, thin legs inconsequential
as Jerry Mahoney's, formerly full, white head
of Irish foam hair scarce and retreating back
into the skull from which it bloomed.

The cemetery full of boat names,
Murphys and Donahues, lacks the
Polish alphabet of reasons my ancestors possess
in their own private hunting grounds
just north of Houdini.
Joseph, your brother, lies patiently
at your father's bare feet, himself
a small shadow of an alternative ending,
wings folded, carefully diapered
in the way they diapered babies
fifty years ago, not having lived long enough
to smile, to see his father's purple irises
wave like an ocean of mercy across
their small Pennsylvania yard.

Joseph, it is your turn now
to feed him the candy bars,
help him grow strong and desirable.
Your mother is here, and on this end,
we will keep her busy, keep her from
needles and alcoholic rainbows,
until the time comes to make the hole
a little wider, accepting into it
one more lily of this man's field. ❋

An Uneventful Life

Linda Melick

The banana that never got ripe
the rice that never got cooked
the arugula that never got eaten.
My life is measured out
in incidents that did not occur.

My daughter always says,
"that's not going to happen."
What does that mean?
Does she know
something I don't?

The man I never married
wrote me a letter from
the rain forest
of Central America.
He said that at his farewell
party when he saw
Italian sausages
floating in the sauce I made,
he almost asked
me to marry him

I could never write back
to him because he had no
address, but I would have
said no because I loved
someone else,
who never loved me. ❀

Ilse's Sleep

Nancy Willard

In Bangall, in a house in a forest, how patiently
Ilse waits for sleep, a shy animal, to arrive.
How everything frightens it. The breath of a bird
at three, the crack of a twig at four.
She in whom cats confide cannot call it.
She who applauds the moon's rising, she who draws
the moon from a well and sprinkles moonwater
on the one hundred and two pots of anemones

in her garden, cannot draw it.
What is to be done? Her husband reads to her.
Poems. Novels. History. What does her sleep
know of history? His voice swabs away letters
unwritten, tasks undone. His voice cleanses,
folds, puts away. When her sleep arrives,
it looks over its shoulder for the secret
police and licks its wounds from the dark

days in Berlin, days of making paper
and printing passports for Jews,
hidden like stars at noon; horses
dead in the streets; a dead boy leaning
against an apple tree blossoming
for the girl whose sleep saw everything
and buried it, but carries it to her now,
in a house in a forest, in Bangall. ❋

Drylands

Claire McGuire

My nerves are dry reeds. They cough his name
in the lightest breeze,
they rub together.

Sparks or stars in the hot night, we crackle like
lightning along the riverbed.

The sun casts down her eyes,
and turns the river to cracked clay.
The wheat dries and dies in the fields.

She will starve us out. No haystacks
lining the paths home, the animals
have all moved on.

Our love is an empty barn,
with dust rising in shafts towards the light.

I Said Coffee

Sharmagne Leland-St. John

I said coffee
I didn't say,
"would you
like to cup
my warm
soft breasts
in your
un-calloused,
long,
tapered,
ringless fingered
hands?"

I said coffee
I didn't say,
"would you
like to
run your tongue
along my neck
just below
my left ear-lobe?"

I said coffee
I didn't say,
"would you
like to
hold me
in your arms
and feel my heart
skip beats
as you press your
hard, lean body
up against mine
until I melt
into you
with desire?"

I said coffee
as we stood there
in the jasmine
scented night
my car door
like some modern day
bundling board
separating us,
protecting us
from ourselves
and lust

I said,
"would you
like to go for
a cup of coffee?"
I didn't say,
"would you
like to brush
your lips
across mine
as you move
silently
to bury your face
in my long, silky,
raven black hair?"

But you said,
"I can't
I'm married
I can't trust myself
to be alone
with you."
So I looked you
dead in the eye
and repeated
"I said coffee" ✳

Valentine

Josepha Gutelius

I write long letters to the dead (you only know how heartfully),
in the woods, scratching the bark with my lonely fantasies, you
were always near, the one to decipher my messages.
True, I would guide you,
you couldn't have found your way alone. I wouldn't
have wanted you to. I loved holding the secret.

It's been thirteen years to the day since your last letter came,
a forest fell out of the envelope, fire blew off the bush, you see
I do remember and handwriting like someone opening his veins.
The charms you enclosed ("spitted flames") looked like the rubies
my mother piled on for shopping tennis anywhere anytime
she didn't give a hoot for propriety.
They kiss-kiss when I put them on.

But that's not what I wanted to say. I'm writing you because
she died yesterday I think you should know that
she kept on asking me *When for godsake you*
going to marry that boy
so handsome and lucky.
I didn't have it in me
to remind her you were dead.

So darling, should you meet her, I'm afraid
you have a little explaining to do.
I meant no harm by my deception, tell her that please,
and let me know
what she says because I hate to think this
is something you can't read. ❋

By All In Me That Curdled
Not In Acid Times   *Christine Boyka Kluge*

By all in me that curdled not in acid times,
by all in me that withered not at heart's parched noon,
I summon you from your lair.

Bring me your scarred hands, your soot-stained fingertips.
Bring me your borrowed body, your new arms, your bright tattoos.
By all in me that longs to trace their ink, word and pattern,
I will know you, and know you are alive.

By all in me neglected by the tiny teeth of time,
by all in me spared by hatred and barbed strife,
by all in me un-plundered — safe from the pirate flag!
I gather my powers and call.

Bring me your singed scent, the hot sun of your intention.
But also the cold moon trapped inside your head.
Bring me the gold constellations a-swirl in your eyes,
stars that burned me from afar when we met.

By all in me dulled not by dull seasons,
by all in me that continues to shine –
by my pointed flame, by the glittering hook of me,
I pull you toward me.

Bring me the fierce brow that softens when you see me.
Bring me your unexpected sweetness as well as your bitter secrets.
Bring me your lips. Yes, bring me your eager lips.

By the truth in me untwisted by sugared lies,
by all in me unbroken, wild and wise —
I summon you from your lair.

Bring me your uncoiling energy, your blue electricity.
Meet me at the body's edge, where boundaries refuse to hold.
Find me where we surge and gleam.
Bring me your eyes with their far-flung stars of gold. ❉

PART 5

SELF in
the WORLD

So Much World

Leslie LaChance

> *So much world all at once—how it rustles and bustles!*
> —Wisława Szymborska,
> "Birthday"

So much world on this little desk – a dictionary!
A blue pen & lime green notebook. Vodka & soda.

The radio plays old jazz and lamplight trembles with the bass line.
Someone is frying garlic down the hall, and of course, below
now, a train. We're

all going somewhere tonight or staying home. We're alone, or not,
sleeping
or wishing we could be, with someone beside us. And the dust!
Everywhere.

Our books in precarious stacks, our cats licking their paws, our
dogs licking
our hands, we're full of supper or starving, on our third glass of
wine, on

the phone with mother. The children are doing their maths or
practicing clarinet.
In the next apartment, the television is not loud enough to cover
our neighbor's

sobs or sounds of lovemaking. No one asked for any of this, but
here it is, and here we are, all at once. ❀

Paper Thin   *Marilyn Reynolds*

In Sesshu's long scroll sea merges with sky
  calligraphic brushstrokes
  suspended in the void   *cranes flying in falling snow*
      Far Eastern paintings teach us
      that paper is not 2-D   but infinite space
      which fits my passion
      to avoid fancy footwork   upon the surface
      to trust my obsession
      to carve images   into and out of a page
      allowing thoughts to breathe in open air
      with sculptural presence
      Short of incising stone
      or digging into a tablet of clay
      I am at the mercy of a medium
      so foreign to me
      that every   arrangement of letters   linear pattern of words
      causes me to pause in uncertainty
      I write   because I am alone
      in the headiness of my life
      I can no longer bear the pressure of voices
      reverberating at my temple's door
      Opening it   their words scramble to make sense
      but released from panic   hover sanely   in modest huddles
      in space and time   that is their own
At the bottom of each page
I re-enter the silence of Sesshu's rock path
going where it takes me
with the hope of passing a stranger
or being invited to tea
under a common moon ❋

Returning to Earth
(or Rediscovering Neruda)   *Susan Jefts*

It happened on a day I went first
to the woods. It happened on a day
I wore my blue scarf, bought a banana almond muffin
and drank shade grown coffee from Brazil.
    When I thought about my conversation with J
last night at the cafe. Images of rocks and roots
came forth, but also a bird in flight. It happened
    on the day I finished my taxes.

It happened between one thing and another,
a book about the soul and a poem about things —
shoes and metal, tobacco smoke, and salt.
"Many things conspired to tell me the whole story,"
wrote Neruda, "not only those things that leap
    and climb, desire and survive."
There are so many — the brass knob of the door,
the ink on the paper, the delivery truck
in the morning. The fibrous thread
    of my book, the blue of the mailbox,
the stone tablets in the park.
It's the way they sing, it's the way they stay still.
So now, it seems I can't say enough about things.
How they connect me to a string in my body
    that binds me to my soul. How every feeling now
is a stone or a street, tobacco smoke, or salt. ❋

Snow Bunting   *Susan Fox Rogers*

It's a blue-sky, cold November morning as Peter and I walk across
a gravel expanse in East Kingston. Where we walk is the site of a
former brick factory, the land now desolate and open, with views
stretching across the Hudson River. Pools of half frozen water
look a toxic green. This place is close to my home, yet I've never
been here before. There's a reason: It's not beautiful. But it has a
certain fascination, the past lurking in the buildings and oozing
up from the ground. Above all, this is where Peter promises we
will see Snow Buntings.

"They could be right there in the grasses, and you'd never see
them," Peter explains. "We'll find them when we flush them."

"Do we want to flush them?" I ask.

"Don't worry. They will circle around and come back," he
explains.

It seems an odd behavior, but then again that is what people
do as well, flee what feels threatening, then return to the same
spot. I am thinking, of course, of love, how I've made the same
mistake again and again, landing, flying, circling back. Right
now, I am looking around, alert, wondering where I have landed.

I stand four feet behind Peter, taking in his wide gentle shoulders
and narrow hips, long skinny legs in two layers of pants in the near-
winter cold. His red hair is wrapped in a purple balaclava. I have
followed him to this ugly place, and am full of hope.

My hope is to see a bird the size of a pudgy sparrow. The Snow
Bunting breeds in the Arctic then travels south for the winter.
In winter, its wings are the color of the wind-whipped grasses.
What remains distinctive is the white belly. There is nothing out
there so white.

We walk, Peter with his camera in hand, me towing the scope.
At the top of a rocky ridge we look down onto a wide plateau,
which rides the bank of the river.

"This is where I found my life Snow Bunting," Peter says. Birders remember their firsts, like lovers remember first kisses. In that moment of the first kiss, I always think: what are the chances I met this person? The same is true of a bird: what are the chances a bird flies from the Arctic to the Hudson Valley and lands where I will find it? Slim, it seems.

As we walk the edge of this torn piece of rocky land, I admire the views onto the river, north to the Kingston-Rhinecliff bridge, and across to the expanse of forest. We walk past a large cement tower, graffitied near the top.

"Let's go back by the river," I say.

Peter nods in agreement. Thirty steps later we flush a flock of birds. Startled, I step back as the birds flutter up and away.

"Buntings!" Peter calls.

I put my binoculars to my eyes, following them as they fly around the desolate lot, circling and circling. I am grinning like an idiot as I thrill at the way the birds bounce up and down as if suspended on a yo-yo. Seen another way, they are like tumbling snowflakes.

"Come on and land," Peter coaxes.

I follow their movement, spinning on my heels. And then the birds do land about fifty feet from where we are standing. In an instant, they vanish. This, in sparse grass, no more than a foot tall. We walk quietly toward where we saw the flock land. They have vaporized. We walk a few steps further and the birds flush, emerging from the earth like white angels.

I take a breath, then laugh. We move toward the plateau by the river as I meditate on *what are the chances*.

"If you saw your life bunting here, and I saw my life bunting here," I start. Before I can finish my thought, another flock flushes. But these don't circle back to land. They take off across the frothy river, vanishing into gray.

"Where are they going?" I ask, knowing there is no answer.

Peter smiles and shrugs and takes my gloved hand as we walk past a disheveled brick building, painted thick with graffiti. Why did the birds fly off? Why did they land here in the first place? Why is Peter next to me in this desolate spot by the Hudson River, the two of us looking for a pudgy little bird? I can't answer any of these questions. All I know is that where I have landed this morning is a new place, filled with the wondrous sight of those white bellies yo-yoing in flight. ❀

Between Now and Never

Meredith Trede

Come morning a silver skim calms the river.
She wakes in thrall to wandering sorrow:
in the shrinking space between now and never
who will ferry the words away for tomorrow?

She wakes in thrall to wandering sorrow,
all the time in her world sealed up inside.
Who will ferry the words away for tomorrow?
The silenced, the dazzled, the blind, there beside

all the time in her world, sealed up inside.
As current pulls while the swelling tide turns
the silenced, the dazzled, the blind: there, beside
time, in shadow or scrim, so silence returns

as current pulls, while the swelling tide turns
in the shrinking space between now and never.
Time in shadow, or scrim, so silence returns.
Come, morning. A silver skim calms the river. ❋

The Valley of the Kings   *Heather Hewett*

I peered at the itinerary clipped onto my handlebars and read the name: "Abbaye de Pontleroy." In front of us, the sign read *"Fermé."* "Strike two," my husband said, getting back onto his bike.

We had left Montrichard that morning, planning to tour some of the Loire Valley's lesser-known castles. It was late September, after the high season — still good for biking but not, apparently, for smaller tourist destinations. First a château and now the abbey: both closed. To make matters worse, after four hours of cycling, we still hadn't found lunch.

I was beginning to regret our decision to explore places that barely merited any mention in our guidebook. We were traveling by bike because we wanted to resist the impulse that so often compels us to visit five cities in five days but then leaves us exhausted and irritable. What better way than a bike, we reasoned, for slowing down? And where better to slow down than in the Loire Valley, where France's kings built their magnificent summer homes?

Yet after miles of pedaling along meandering roads, my stomach wished we weren't moving quite so slowly.

At the next village, we headed straight for the sole restaurant in our guidebook. Closed. Sighing, we pushed on.

At 2 o'clock, the hour when lunch in France usually ends, we reached a small town. Newly built, compact houses and piles of fresh dirt: It must have been built yesterday, because it wasn't on our map. A small sign announced its name: Feings. We arrived at a nondescript brick building with lace-curtained windows and a chalkboard with the day's menu. *Voilà!*

A few customers still lingered, smoking cigarettes and bantering with the bartender. We sat down at a tidy table, and a waiter brought us fresh bread and steamed mussels. We ordered a carafe of the house white wine and dove into our feast, eating each course placed in front of us—savory duck, pungent goat cheese, and the perfect *tarte Tatin* for dessert. The sugary apples and flaky crust melted in my mouth.

The chef emerged from the kitchen, smiling at our empty plates. We thanked him and contentedly rubbed our satisfied stomachs. At last we paid our bill—the cost of one sandwich and a Coke in Manhattan—and drifted back out into the warm sun, ready to explore.

We biked past old stone houses trimmed with red flowers and thick with ivy.

At the edge of town, we came to a field of fading sunflowers. The blackened, bowed heads startled me. They weren't at all what you see on postcards, and yet somehow, they were still majestic. Towering beside the road, they looked like elderly kings humbly shedding their crowns. It was autumn, after all, and the summer tourist season was over; now was the time for harvesting grapes and drinking new wine.

The sunflowers swayed gently in the wind. And now we biked as slowly as we could, reveling in the majesty of the Valley of the Kings. ❀

Surprisingly Wild   *Ruth D. Handel*

Whatever drops from the tree
to the bench where I sit reading
lands — a soft thud —
in the middle of a poem
and holds its place.

A lacewing.
Purposeful,
needle-thin body,
oval translucent wings.
Two pairs.
Delicately traced.
A slow pulse
near its head draws a shadow
on the white.

I had been reading
about a surprisingly
wild urban park
when the lacewing found me.
We look at the page together,
its body dark underline.
I am content to read the poem
over and over.
Be still, Kafka said,
and the world will come to you.
When I bend to see its eyes,
the lacewing flies off. ❋

Reminder in the Midst of Traffic   *Janice P. Egry*

A pile of bone and fur
thrown by rubber and steel
to a permanent spot
in gravel and weeds,
insides pleading out,
white tail lifting
from the whiz of passing cars.

She saw the green meadow
on the other side,
saw her babies there
waiting to be fed.
The deer didn't know
her destiny was tossed,
crows already perched in trees,
also hoping for nourishment. ❋

Azure Aubade

Pamela Hart

Through the window the blue
Of you breaks among boney maples

Your arrival in notes of early light
Is departure, your echo an entrance

Dressed in lapis, like skin you're
Here before there's time to forget

Your cobalt speaks
Hawk or heat wave

You turn Prussian then aqua
At turquoise you're gone to noon

You ink the Nile, in Kabul
Eyes capture your cerulean folds

My day is cadmium mellow
A surfeit of blank, I lose you

In lichen, you're Mary's Cloak
Neptune, Ella at the Cote D'Azur

A flash of your electric
Blue snags feather then vein

Which contains me till evening
Your indigo return inspiring night ❋

Turtle Commute   *Caroline Wolfe*

She knows no other way
    hones toward home
        pilgrimage to patch of sand and mud in sun

                to the wetlands to lay her eggs

Eighteen-wheeler idles at the stop light
            death roulette
            she never agreed to play

Traffic hazards pulse, I dash across
        highway divider lines
            to save her life this one time

              Winter pond left behind, she presses
on

Dense armor shell, carapace defense
    attack, vicious jaws, snap
            cadaver claws rip toward my innards

I carry her, heavy and heaving
        across black pavement,
            hold tight, murderous eyes

                Set her safely on the other side

She steps toward sand and mud in sun
        another season within
            this is her way, she knows no other ❋

The Swimming Hole   *Laura Shaine Cunningham*

It has been in the news this week: The swimming hole is now officially closed to the public.

It seems odd to read about the swimming hole, as if the contents of my most private dresser drawer were inventoried on the front page of the newspaper. The swimming hole seemed personal, if not private. I have been swimming there for twenty summers. I know the cave behind the "Little Falls," the cool stone room, curtained by the gush of white water, a place where it is said many local girls lost their virginity, and where the occasional beer can testifies that forbidden fun still occurs there, unseen ...

It is a local game to dive from the falls. There are tales of fellows with "steel plates" in their foreheads. Jumping from above, it is possible to hit the "hole" from the top of the falls, but it is also easy to miss. One long ago summer afternoon, I saved a boy from drowning there—he was one of the teen daredevils, and he missed a step. He stood for a moment, arms akimbo, wavering. His balance lost, he tried to walk the silken crown of the fall to cross it like a wirewalker. I was sitting on the rock beside the fall, on an outcropping. Without planning to, I reached out and steadied him, led him back to the rock. He didn't thank me. He went back to a boom box that blared a song I hated, at a volume I resented. He avoided me the rest of that hot day, as if, by saving him, I had also committed a faux pas of the swimming hole.

I was there during a heat wave, when I couldn't see the rocks for the people sitting on them: a flesh-colored cliff of people. The Creek became a town on water—music played, people carried coolers so heavy, they seemed to require porters.

A young man dove, wearing only a loincloth. "Tarzan!" Everyone yelled. No one knew his real name. He had a Fabio-like blond mane, and a chamois loincloth. He was built, as they say. It was diverting ....

The water, while always a cooling gush, is often not that attractive; sometimes, a brown froth rises, the "townie" debris littered the shoreline: hardened socks, lost shorts, stiffened in the mud, condom rings and a zillion flip-tops. A shallow archeological dig into our present. Sometimes, on a hot afternoon, the swimming hole could seem sordid ... even the rocks got too hot, and all I'd note was the cigarette butts, in the puddles that filled the dimples of the stone "beach."

For every ugliness, there were a thousand beauties: the osprey that dove and screamed, coming up successful with the brown trout in her beak. The herons, so narrow, one could imagine them an illusion, skimming the water, looking too, for the fish that seemed like wingless shadows of the birds above. At dawn, all was always delightful; toward dusk the magic light: Purple loosestrife against the sky-reflecting waters. All is blue, purple, green ...

There was always drama: My daughter, on her first tiptoe in the water, at age three, was caressed (and that's the word) by a six foot corn snake that slithered past, then seemed to chase us, as we ran screaming back onto the shore: The snake passed us: she was heading elsewhere, leaving us jumping up on logs, cartooning ourselves. The Rondout Creek was never what you expected — in heavy rain, it swelled silver, slashing trees in its path. This week, it will be gentle, and the raspberries will ripen within reach.

There are many factors that have closed the swimming hole, and the law is an attempt to end the drama that has taken place here. Last summer, a boy from Queens came up, dove, and missed. He died. The power company has lied; this is not the park they promised. The "stone beach" is sold to a private owner, now beleaguered by a town that wants to "swim in." All that is dangerous and alluring about the swimming hole is being exposed this summer. The tidal wave of a future coming at us has sucked back the past and left us looking at our present. ❋

A Part of Life   *Micky Shorr*

Springtime in Venice Beach—salt smell in the morning air.
Sense of landing somehow in this easy place, worlds away
from urban hardships.

I'm making a baby, thus far, enjoying it immensely. Happily
imagine the soon to be blessed event where I will, according
to the Boyer method, simply breathe that baby out.

Now it happens. It's downtown L.A., the medical center,
taking lots more time than I expected. I long for some sleep,
hear screams nearby, want to call the whole thing off.

Instead, they whisk me down the hall to a chilled florescent place.
Space not unlike a room they wheel me years later. Another growth,
this one most dreaded.

Same stark coldness of the table, same eyes on the masked physician.
There where death and breath collide. ❁

War

Kateri Kosek

When he first leaves
she carries her blank notebook to the fields
and spends entire days there, stealing apples
from the orchard. Everything
she admires is attached
to the hard certainty of him
and the possibility of his return:
morning light filtered through a stand of birches,
crushed green of the world after a rainstorm,
clouds over the hills towards evening
that go orange in the last shard of sun.
She wishes she knew how to draw the light.

※ ※ ※

The birds have begun to move south.
Once her father told her they fly all night; sometimes
their silhouettes cross the moon. She can't sleep so
she goes out, watches for a while.
A nighthawk cuts the sky just above her head,
wings pointed in sporadic flight,
uncertain in its direction and flying no farther
than the other side of the field.

※ ※ ※

When she learns he's not coming back
she joins the farmhands in their harvesting,
abandons her book, anchors herself
to soil and roots and corn. She learns
not to think more than necessary.
The harsh contours of the hills in winter
are not particularly devastating.
When she begins to draw the birches out her window,

they are only birches, a series of shapes and curves—
no inherent possibility in their clean slender trunks,
the way they cage the light. ✳

Thursday's Child

Ethel Wesdorp

You slipped from the shadows
Your hand outstretched
Pasted smile on your face
Wearing fatigues like a business suit.

You called out to my friend,
"Will you give me a hand?
An Iraqi Vet, from the VA,
Need twenty more for a ticket home."

My friend, A Vietnam Vet,
Another Generation, another War,
Turned away, refusing his plea,
"Can't help you," was all he said.

The elevator doors hissed apart,
Without a word we stepped inside,
We rode down to the underground.
"You never can tell": the epilogue.

I wonder if you still wander there,
Haunting the halls in your fatigues;
Did you ever make it home again?
Did you have far to go? ❋

Holes He Digs

Teresa Sutton

His tongue can lick the base of his brain, that grey matter
that's turned a dark shade in the deep space of dendrites
that's gone black.

There, Christopher Columbus just now discovers Hispaniola,
light years away from American History and nuns with thick rulers,
beyond the edge of the visible universe.

His F51-D Mustang prop plane takes off from Kansas
and slides through another wormhole in search of the rhythm
of the world where he used to live.

Time is that plane that transforms into a bird above an ocean
full of photos of boys and girls, men and women, familiar,
yet slippery as schools of fish that glint and dart
right below the moving surface.

Space is the barren landscape where craters in the brain's tissue
meet basins and canyons on yet to be named planets,
where platoons of microbes spill into cups from spigots
left to run on and on.

When the fingernail of his pinky scrapes away
the last of his eardrum, air rushes into the blackness,
into these holes to fan the slow fire in the cortex.

He sails away on the Santa Maria bound again for the Korean War,
then he hops aboard the Nina and heads off to the dinner table
where he pours himself a glass of water that's full of ash. ❋

every day is 9/11   *Trina Porte*

what you don't get is
his body never stops
landing on you

ask a soldier
from any other kind of war
they know it too

birds sing
the sun comes up
another glorious day begins

and it flashes through your mind
another thousand times
whether your heart races

or you've learned how
to keep breathing
slow steady breaths

as you force yourself to look
out the window
instead of seeing him

invade your eyes
closed or open, awake or asleep
and the fucking television

says take a pill
buy something pretty
stop being a victim

it happened so long ago
but what they don't know is
it's never over ✸

i am another yourself *   *Deborah Poe*

the cliffs cut between two countries
displace agitation between two hemispheres
such mountainous territories of mind

there is luxury to write this
(the baking, the sleeping, the shooting)
by the time you've read this, quadrillions of signals fire

there's no soul, no twenty-one grams
what's left? brain, two percent of the body's weight,
seizes a chunk of the body's oxygen and bolts

at a museum, the Ferrari's plaque
reads aluminum and titanium
not watercolor, acrylic, or oil

the nervous system trajects information
like heart circulates your blood
nerves, bone, and steel — objects we have in common

below the bridge (which could always be blown up) —
in the last few seconds what you and I remember
relies on synapses, mental acts, artifacts

fresh tortillas, front yard, the writing on the wall. ❀

*In Lak'ech, the Mayan Code of Honor, I am another yourself

Draft Me a Space
in Your Harbor
Adrianna Delgado

Draft me a space in your harbor
A retreat far from the civilized wind, cold and uncaring
Free me from winter shells of war
Free me from the scars of sky scraped ice,
from the diseased blood of the Sycamore
Torn down and bare
No longer rustling or raring for change in color
Leaves ravaged to the ground before their last Fall
Please, draft me a space in your harbor
Before Death rips tears out of clay ships
Before clay ships sail to nether worlds
and I arrive far from my true origin forgetting the way back home ❈

Sleeping Buddha   *Sarah Gardner*

As the train rolled out of Lanzhou, a mixed-voice quartet was
singing Brahms' lullaby in Chinese over the loudspeakers. The train
ambled along and the city persisted for miles. Lanzhou, Lanzhou,
Lanzhou, the massive pastel apartment blocks that look alike in
every quarter of the city, then rail yards, military trains on sidings,
bald tan mountains in the near distance, a glimpse of the gleaming
northwestern suburb from afar. Factories, then Lanzhou turning
low-rise, with squat and shabby apartment blocks that gave way to
miles of big truck and heavy equipment dealers. Fuel tanks, more
factories, the Yellow River visible, mountains looming closer. We
crossed the Yellow River and were instantly in the countryside.
Every little farmstead had its own enclosed compound, a wall as
high as the buildings themselves. There was a haystack in every
courtyard and a satellite dish on every rooftop. Farm fields stretched
to the mountains' feet. I marveled that anything could grow in
soil that looked like dirty talcum powder. After nearly a year of
residence, my understanding of China was taking shape like the
image on a paint-by-numbers canvas. Tiny dabs of color gradually
interlocked and merged, forming something almost recognizable.
  My destination this time was Zhangye, about five hundred
miles northwest of my teaching post in Lanzhou, Gansu. Unlike
Lanzhou, the sprawling provincial capital, Zhangye is a small
rural town—so small that it is possible to walk anywhere within
its limits in minutes. On my first morning, I was sitting in a
noodle shop enjoying breakfast, looking out the open door at the
sunlit street and thinking how bucolic it all was, when a man
walked by leading a cow. Later that morning I was strolling on
Marco Polo Street in the town's eager, garish, nearly-deserted
new commercial district. A young man greeted me and we began
to walk along together. He introduced himself as Du Hei Qi, a
middle school teacher and lover of English who would like me to

be his "American friend" and teach him my language. I explained
that I was on a brief visit, so it wouldn't be possible for me to be
his tutor. When we reached my hotel, I shook his hand and said
good-bye. Little did I know that when I emerged later, he would
be waiting for me. My plan was to explore the town on foot
in welcome solitude. Instead, I saw the sights in the relentless
company of my new friend.

He had exhausted his fund of English and I, my Chinese during
our first meeting, so the next hours were spent walking in silence
or revisiting old topics.

"Do you like China?"

"Yes, I like China very much."

"Is America a beautiful country?"

"Yes, America is very beautiful"

The Chinese word for America, 美国, translates literally
to "beautiful country." I gently declined tea, a meal, and even
an invitation to take a nap in his room. Finally I accepted his
invitation to have our portrait taken together in a photo studio.
The photographer unfurled a brilliant green backdrop depicting
grass, trees, and an English country cottage with a white picket
fence. We stepped together into the idyllic two-dimensional world,
the camera's flash capturing our fleeting friendship. A day later,
the hotel desk clerk handed me an envelope containing a crisply
laminated print. I felt guilty and sad. Du Hei Qi was beaming;
I towered over him looking harassed, the neckline of my blouse
askew, hands clasped nervously before me, my strained smile
showing how eager I was to free myself of his cloying presence.

It rained lightly for half of the following day. It was a marvel; it
seldom rains in Gansu in the spring. The whole town took on the
flat, metallic smell of wet dust. When the rain let up, I set out
to see the Sleeping Buddha, Zhangye's principle attraction. Over
thirty meters long, this is the largest reclining Buddha in China.
The Buddha and his entire temple were propped up and filled

with scaffolding. A 2003 earthquake had damaged the shrine, and restoration was still in process.

All the same, I could gaze upon his lovely toes and his massive chest blazoned with the swastika. I hadn't known until I came to China that Hitler had co-opted that Buddhist symbol of peace; it always startled me to see it in a sacred setting. Buddha's eyes were half closed as he glided ever closer to Nirvana; his full lips tilted in a gentle, dreamy smile. Despite its stylized form and garish colors, the face looked sublimely peaceful. In my mind, a Chinese quartet was singing Brahms' lullaby in perfect harmony. Not for the first time, or the last, I glimpsed the ying and the yang: the frenetic, grasping hospitality of modern China against the backdrop of its deeply tranquil ancient culture. ✳

The Powder Tower   *Michelle Woods*

My grandmother and I walk toward the Powder Tower on a hot
day spackled with dust. Prague is a heap of cobblestones and
abandoned wheelbarrows; the metro is being birthed under our
feet. I'm being pulled, not reluctantly, just, I'm too small. My
grandmother has that fierce look on her face, a tightly lipsticked
grimace under a tightly dyed Marcel wave. She always wears
slacks, elegant and utterly fashionable in 1939. That's the year her
and my grandfather's fashions end. Don't ask me what year it is
now; I'm too small. Time comes in bursts and vanishes.

The Powder Tower is dun-colored but soot-covered so that
it merges upward into its black gothic roof. Its small windows,
flecks of gold, and wide arch at its bottom give it a face, the
mansard roof is a dapper hat. Kings used it to gate the city, store
their gunpowder, but its mouth is open now and the city built
itself through it. Look behind you! But it has no neck, it can't
turn, and what's behind it was a future, once.

We walk toward the Powder Tower. Always. On Hybernská
Street. A musket shot of a memory. After the smoke, the
gunpowder, we vanish. Sometimes there's a brief flash of a
shop — wooden floor, wooden shelves — almost entirely empty.
Me and Babi are in there and some hands, never a face, cover a
package with paper, tie twine around it with a little finger hole so
you can dangle it on the way home on an index finger. The paper
is cheap, coarse woodchips are pitted in it, the twine rough and
itchy. But it's tied with elegance, time taken to make it something
you open slowly and tenderly. Don't ask me what's in it. Not a
toy, and not food. I would have remembered.

Kafka says something about the shades of the dead lapping
at the water of the Acheron because of the salt of our seas. The
river recoils, washing the dead back to life. The tides, then,
are strange, lapping at dust and vanishing, unasked for, moving

to their own strange internal rhythms. Babi washes back in, thirsty with salt. And we walk toward the Powder Tower. On Hybernská Street. Past the Café Arco, abandoned now, where Kafka sat. "I can't really remember your face in any precise detail," he writes from there to his lover, Milena Jesenská. "Only the way you walked away through the tables in the café, your figure, your dress, that I still see." Milena is also Babi's name. Miloushka. From the Czech verb for love.

Babi is astonishingly beautiful and malevolently petulant. She is guarded by glassy-eyed black poodles, all named after delicate flowers, with sharp teeth consistently aimed at baby flesh. We keep our hands on the lace tablecloth by the china cups and saucers, and we bunch in our feet, never quite on the chairs, out of range of their patrolling jaws. Azalia is the queen, Azalka, fed with a spoon, her pink tongue darting out between her fangs, her black curls, and her blacker eyes.

Děda, my roly-poly grandfather, almost a perfect physical circle, sits. He sits and listens, sits and sleeps, sits and eats, lets me sit on him. He walks in brown trousers pulled up to his chest, a brown overcoat and a brown trilby. His habit is to raise his hat to every lady he passes, but he can't now. I hold one of his hands, my brother his other, and we've just squeezed off the metro at the Main Station. The Prague Metro has opened today! We travel one stop.

No one wants him to take us. His heart! Babi yells. His diabetes! my aunt yells. It's okay! my mother yells, and we sneak out under the yelling, the three of them in the kitchen right at the center of the apartment. It is square, the apartment, but seems round, like Děda. Each room opens into another, scalloped lace curtains blowing in from the casement windows, blowing in the dust, until you end up back at the hall.

I saw them in a handful of visits three, four years apart. It was hard to get through the walls of the city, now gated by politics and official spite. Děda died; Babi claimed to go blind. She wrote letters with Sharpie pens, thick black bitter marks. "Přestaň!" she snapped at me — stop it! — once when I waddled into her peripheral vision, a Tiresias of terror. Why do we keep walking toward the Powder Tower and then vanish? Babi is not even a shade, but a barking, biting smudge.

What's left of her is a letter to her daughters, Yvonka (9 months old, my mother) and Renatka (3 years old, in hiding). A testament of the war, a circular narrative of transports, Děda's family vanishing in waves. Babi saves Děda's life; those in "mixed marriages" went last. They married in 1939, so the Nazis turn Babi into a Jew. She will not have it, stamps her petulant foot, and demands to be an Aryan again. Still, they starve. Terry, their dog, is taken away ("They did not even overlook the animals."). Yvonka and Renatka are put on the transport list ("I thought that night of suicide."), but at the last minute Yvonka is spared, Renatka spirited away.

Babi brings Děda to the transport. He could not lift his trilby. "The heavy bag on his back, the knapsack in front, his coat in his hands, his bent back and such pain in his heart." "We didn't talk much to each other," she wrote, "rather we said a lot with our eyes." Writing the letter, she does not know if he is alive. Děda, who sits and listens, sits and sleeps, sits and eats, escapes — *escapes* — from Terezín. No one knows how; the story vanishes. Děda sits and smiles. I like to think Babi stamped her foot, the earth shook, and he rolled all the way home.

We walk to the Powder Tower, the fierce lipstick, the tight Marcel wave, the dust. ❋

How to Make Your Mother Laugh   *Lucia Cherciu*

Even after living in a different country
for seventeen years,
I read my home-town paper twice a week,
collect stories,
details about the price of milk,
and learn that you can translate salaries
internationally
in numbers of chickens.

A woman left her three children
home alone for seven days,
all between two and six years old;
when they were found
they were eating cardboard,
huddled together for heat.

A couple sold one of their children
in France for a ticket home.
A woman abandoned her four-year old daughter
in a corner of a cemetery
in gray-black winter.

A highly-educated woman,
showed in a picture
as very attractive and trendy,
killed her mother
by suffocating her with a pillow
then hanged herself from a pipe.

Then I call my mother
and we laugh together.
She tells me
that Lelea Irina from our village
got on the bus to see her daughter
for Christmas
but somehow never arrived. ❋

Crushed in Poughkeepsie Time   *Lea Graham*

> *What is seen here/folding over itself/*
> *is a gathering of those /pasts we voyage into*
> —MICHAEL ANANIA'S
> "The River Songs of Arion, I-X"

Whale-rending along these shores leads us to South Seas,
a silk factory, hotel burnings; like dreams' net or currents
one with another— hemlock-black, brackish & lovely, fresh

or tang, estuary's switch. That all time cannot exist at once
in our heads: cigar-making & electric trolleys, how you bent
& sighed into your shoes, peeled oranges in the shape

of eyes. What is forgotten lingers, the "lion-headed store front,"
bobs or busts through this *now*, a warning without warning,
can you dig it, a buoy of the past, place-marker

& maker, tricked out as "picking your feet"
in *The French Connection,* cough drops called "Trade" & "Mark,"
rising high school rafters in Marian Andersen's contralto.

Imagine histories current: ferries trawl nigh 300 years;
Brando haunts Happy Jack's on Northbridge Street.
We might say *Poughkeepsie* & hear "reed-covered lodge

near the place of the little-water," "the Queen City,"
"safe & pleasant harbor," *look* & see the Pequod chief
& his beloved spooning in the shade. This river sailing the Half-

Moon back to Crusades, a city spelled 42 ways & young Vassar
brewing in Newburgh. Rio San Gomez is the Mauritius
is the Muheakantuck is the Lordly Hudson, place of the

deepest water & river of the steep hills— what if we are still
dancing in Chicago's hottest summer as Wappingi braves
are coming up the path & Van Kleek's house just

yonder Fall Kill? You are writing me letters from Rio Dulce
& I am eating bagels at the Reo Diner. Modjeski sits imagining
this bridge; his mother swoons as Juliet in Crakow.

At night the lights of these still busy foundries become
strange fires, beckoning America—& maybe not;
their great furnaces' ambient noise, soughing across these

waters; concurrent worlds asleep, dreaming, not dreaming ✳

The Editors

Laurence Carr is a writer of plays, fiction and poetry. His novel, *Pancake Hollow Primer, A Hudson Valley Story*, published by Codhill Press, won first prize at the 2012 Next Generation Indie Book Awards for First Novel (under 80,000 words). He is the editor of *Riverine: An Anthology of Hudson Valley Writers* and the co-editor of *WaterWrites: A Hudson River Anthology*, also from Codhill. His fiction and poetry has been published throughout the United States. Over 20 of his plays and theatre pieces have been produced in New York City, regionally, and in Europe; they include *Vaudeville*, *The Voyage of Mary C.*, *36 Exposures*, and *Hamlet's Lear*. He received a B.F.A. from Ohio University and a Master's Degree from The Gallatin School of Individualized Study at New York University. He teaches Dramatic and Creative Writing at SUNY, New Paltz. carrlarry@optonline.net.

Jan Zlotnik Schmidt is a SUNY Distinguished Teaching Professor and a member of the English Department at SUNY New Paltz where she teaches composition, creative writing, American and Women's Literature, creative nonfiction, memoir, and Holocaust literature courses. Her work has been published in many journals including *The Cream City Review, Kansas Quarterly, The Alaska Quarterly Review, Home Planet News, Phoebe, Black Buzzard Review, The Chiron Review, and Wind*. Her poetry also has been nominated for the Pushcart Press Prize Series. She has had two volumes of poetry published by the Edwin Mellen Press (*We Speak in Tongues*, 1991; *She had this memory, 2000*). Recently a chapbook, *The Earth Was Still*, was published by Finishing Line

Press (2011). In addition to her poetry publications, she has edited two anthologies of women's memoirs (*Women/Writing/Teaching* [SUNY Press 1998] and, with Dr. Phyllis R. Freeman, *Wise Women: Reflections of Teachers at Mid-Life* [Routledge 2000]). Her literature for composition anthology, *Legacies: Fiction Poetry Drama Nonfiction*, co-edited with Dr. Carley Bogarad (deceased) and Dr. Lynne Crockett, is now in its fifth edition.

THE CONTRIBUTORS

Edie Abrams received her Master's from Rensselaer Polytechnic Institute. Edie participates in the Every-Other-Thursday poetry workshop in Voorheesville. She co-hosts Sunday Four Poetry Open Mic and the Smith's Tavern Poet Laureate Contest. Rootdrinker Institute's Benevolent Bird Press published Edie's chapbook, *Mermaid in Metamorphosis*. *The River Reporter* published "Sweet Autumn Clematis."

Barbara Adams has published two books of poetry, *Hapax Legomena* and *The Ordinary Living;* a book of literary criticism, *The Enemy Self: Poetry and Criticism of Laura Riding;* and a memoir, *The Stone Man and the Poet* (2011). She won the 2007 Robert Frost Foundation Award for her poem, "Henry Jones, from Wales." Her story, "Portrait of the Artist's Daughter," won First Prize in the 1999 *Negative Capability* Fiction Contest. She is a retired professor emerita of English at Pace University.

Jacqueline Renee Ahl is currently the Specialist for Disabilities and Learning at SUNY New Paltz and an instructor for the Summer Institute for the Gifted at Vassar College. Her stage plays have earned three national and international awards and have been produced in the Hudson Valley, New York City, North Carolina, and Montana.

Brittany Ambrosio found her passion for writing as early as grade school. She was chosen for a selective writing program at a young age. She took creative writing workshops throughout her grade school and college career. In her senior year of high school, two poems were published in her school's literary magazine, *Revelations.*

Nava Atlas is best known for her bestselling vegan and vegetarian cookbooks; however, she also produces visual nonfiction, most recently, *The Literary Ladies' Guide to the Writing Life* (2011). Nava is also an artist (navaatlasart.com) whose work is shown across the United States. She is at work on a graphic biography.

Carol Yuen Bean is primarily interested in using poetry as a means for articulating that which is not given space in the course of a typical day. Her aim is to explore communication as communion and to bear witness to a life that has suddenly turned delightful.

Sylvia Barnard was born in 1937 in Greenfield, Massachusetts and has written poetry all her life. In1959, she published a book in the McGill Poetry Series. She has taught Latin, Greek, and ancient civilization for forty-four years at SUNY Albany.

Celia Bland's work has recently appeared in *Hoppenthaler's Congeries, The Narrative Review* (where her poem, Wasps," was named one of the year's best), and *Drunken Boat,* and will appear in *In/Filtration, Word For/Word*, and *The Virginia Quarterly Review. The Madonna Comix,* a collaboration with the artist Dianne Kornberg, will be published in 2013.

Sally Bliumis-Dunn teaches Modern Poetry and Creative Writing at Manhattanville College. She received her B.A. in Russian language and literature from U.C. Berkeley in 1983 and her MFA in Poetry from Sarah Lawrence College in 2002. In 2002, she was a finalist for the Nimrod/Hardman Pablo Neruda Prize. Her poems have been published in *The Paris Review, Prairie Schooner, Poetry London,* and the *New York Times,* among others. In 2008, she was asked to read in the *Love Poems* program at the Library of Congress. She lives in Armonk, New York. Her first book, *Talking Underwater,* was published in 2007 by Wind Publications. Her second book, *Second Skin*, was published by Wind Publications in 2010.

Ann Cefola is the author of *St. Agnes, Pink-Slipped* (Kattywompus Press, 2011), *Sugaring* (Dancing Girl Press, 2007) and the translation *Hence This Cradle* (Seismicity Editions, 2007). A Witter Bynner Poetry Translation Residency recipient, she also received the Robert Penn Warren Award judged by John Ashberry.

Amy Cheng (cover art) was born in Taiwan, raised in Brazil, Oklahoma and Texas. She received a BFA from the University of Texas at Austin, and an MFA from Hunter College, City University of New York. She has exhibited her paintings both nationally and internationally and her work is held in a number of corporate and public collections. She received a P.S. 122 Painting Center Fellowship in New York City for a ten month residency in 2011–12, and a Senior Lecture/Research Fulbright fellowship to Brazil in 2008. She has been awarded two New York Foundation for the Arts Painting Fellowships, and an Arts International travel grant to China. She is a Professor in the Art Department at the State University of New York at New Paltz.

Lucia Cherciu is a Professor of English at SUNY /Dutchess. Her poetry appeared in *Connecticut Review, Cortland Review, Memoir (and), Legacies, Spillway,* and elsewhere. Her books of poetry are *Lepa˘darea de Limba˘ (The Abandonment of Language)*: Editura Vinea, 2009, and *Altoiul Râsului (Grafted Laughter)*: Editura Brumar, 2010.

Catharine Clarke has found soulful solace through writing for over 40 years. A single mother in Manhattan for 17 years, she is late to commit fully to her writing life but has recently enjoyed publishing essays, poetry and a short story included in the *Wallkill Valley Writers Anthology.* She is at work on a historical novel.

Suzanne Cleary's *Beauty Mark*, winner of the 2012 John Ciardi Prize for Poetry, will be published by BkMk Press of the University of Missouri-Kansas City. Her previous books are *Keeping Time* and *Trick Pear.* Winner of a Pushcart Prize, she has had her work published in many anthologies and journals.

Brenda Connor-Bey (deceased) was the Poet Laureate for the town of Greenburgh, New York. She was the author of *Thoughts of an Everyday Woman/An Unfinished Urban Folktale*, a member of the Advisory Committees for the Slapering Hol Press, the Westchester Center for Creative Aging, and the Poetry Caravan. A recipient of the Westchester Fund for Women and Girls' Outstanding Arts Educator Award, a NYSCAPS award for poetry, four PEN awards for nonfiction and a NYFA award for fiction, Brenda was a MacDowell YADDO and Cave Canem Regional Fellow.

Teresa Marta Costa recently published *in Ulster Magazine, Stained Sheets, Chronogram, Home Planet News,* and *Riverine,* among others. She has read extensively throughout the Hudson Valley, written a restaurant review for *Home Planet News,* and is currently working on her first book. She hosts poetry readings at Bohemian Book Bin as well as the Woodstock Goddess Poetry Festival, held in March 2012, which supported the Ulster County Battered Women's Shelter.

Lynne Crockett received her Ph.D. in Victorian Literature from New York University and is employed as a professor and Writing Program Administrator at SUNY Sullivan. Crockett writes a monthly column for the *Shawangunk Journal* and has published her creative nonfiction in literary anthologies and journals.

Laura Shaine Cunningham is the author of two memoirs, *Sleeping Arrangements* and *A Place in the Country*, both of which were originally published in *The New Yorker.*

Joann K. Deiudicibus is a writing instructor and the Staff Assistant for the Composition Program at the State University of New York at New Paltz, where she earned her B.A. (2000), and M.A. (2003), both in English. She is the Associate Editor (poetry) for *WaterWrites: A Hudson River Anthology* (Codhill Press) and has been published in *The North Street Journal, Orange Review, Literary Passions, Fortunate Fall, Chronogram,* and *The Shawangunk Review.* Her poetry was selected for The Woodstock Poetry Festival in 2003.

Adrianna Delgado has been reading her work throughout the Hudson Valley, New York City,

Phoenix, Arizona, and Pennsylvania since 2002. Her first chapbook, *All Words are Verbs*, was published in 2012 by YourName Productions. She co-hosts Poetry, Beacon at Bank Square in Beacon and is the editor of the anthology, *Belief Persists*.

Dinah Dietrich writes poetry, fiction, and memoir. She holds a B.A. from Bennington College and an M.A. from the University of Massachusetts, Amherst. Dinah's work has been published in *Recovering the Self: a Journal of Hope and Healing, Berkshire Anthology, Outpost Magazine*, and other literary journals.

Lisa Fleck Dondiego was a semi-finalist in the Discovery contest. Her poems have appeared in *The Westchester Review, Let the Poets Speak, Haibun Today* and Red Moon Press's yearly anthology, *contemporary haibun*. She has read in New York City at the Cornelia St. Café and at the Hudson Valley Writers' Center. Her chapbook, *A Sea of Change*, was published by Finishing Line Press in 2011. She lives in Ossining with her husband.

Janice P. Egry received her B.S. and M.S. from Crane School of Music, University of New York at Potsdam, and is certified in K–12 Special Education. She taught music and special education in public schools before retiring to write full time. Her poems have been published in *Capper's, Writing the Natural Way* (a textbook on writing by Gabriele Rico) and several anthologies. Her poem, "Silence of the Song," was grand prize winner of the Artists Embassy International 2008 Dancing Poetry Contest and Festival in San Francisco.

Betty Ann Enos neé Damms had written children's historical fiction. Her work has been published in *Hudson Valley Mature Life, Chronogram, and Reading Objects* (produced by the Samuel Dorsky Museum of Art at SUNY, New Paltz), and she currently is working on other projects. Her short stories and poems are posted at authorsden.com/BettyAnnDamms.

Mary E. Fakler is a Lecturer in the Department of English at SUNY New Paltz, teaching writing and literature courses. She has presented her research on collaborative writing and learning at national and international conferences and has published in several journals. Her continuing research centers on the Japanese-American internment experience.

Alyssa Fane is a recent graduate of the State University of New York at New Paltz. As a student, she had both a critical essay and a poem published in on-campus literary publications. She also received on-campus awards for creative writing. Currently, she is working on a novel, *Too*, inspired by personal family history.

Alice Feeley has, during the past eighteen years, produced a chapbook and had poems published. She's a member of Westchester's Poetry Caravan; two years ago she was appointed Greenburgh Poet Laureate. In 2011 she initiated POETRY: A DOORWAY TO PRAYER, a program for writers and seekers.

Carole Bell Ford earned her doctorate at Columbia University in 1980. She has taught Women's Studies along with History and Educational Studies at Empire State College. Her books include: *The Girls: Jewish Women of Brownsville, Brooklyn* (SUNY Press, 2000); *The Women of CourtWatch: Reforming a Corrupt Family Court System* (University of Texas Press, 2005) selected by *Justice for Children*, as an outstanding work; and *After the Girls Club: How Teenaged Holocaust Survivors Built New Lives in America* was published in 2010 (Lexington Books).

Penny Freel is currently a lecturer of Composition and Literature in the English Department at SUNY New Paltz. From 1995–2003, she taught at the University of The Sacred Heart in Tokyo, Japan. She was a co-editor of *WaterWrites* (2010), a Hudson River anthology. She enjoys reading her students' writing as well as writing her own stories.

Phyllis R. Freeman is Associate Professor of Psychology and former Dean of The Graduate School at SUNY New Paltz (1999-2004). An experimental psychologist, she has been a college teacher for more than 35 years. Dr Freeman was the Liberal Arts & Sciences Teacher of the Year in 1996-1997 and was named the 2008 SUNY New Paltz Alumni Association Distinguished

Teacher. Dr Freeman is the co-editor with Professor Jan Zlotnik Schmidt of *Wise Women: Reflections of Teachers at Midlife* published by Routledge (2000) among other publications.

Allison B. Friedman is a writer, a practicing psychotherapist, and an active member of the Wallkill Valley Writers Workshop. She has published several short stories in literary journals and wrote a newspaper column oxymoronically entitled "Understanding Adolescence" for the *Poughkeepsie Journal* for many years. She also has been a monthly columnist for *"Living and Being"* magazine, and the host of "The Therapy Sisters," a live radio talk show in Kingston.

Sarah Gardner is an instructor of English who spent the year from 2005 to 2008 teaching at Ganso United University in Lanzhou, People's Republic of China. Her blog, sarahsays.blogspot.com relates her experiences there, as does the essay, "The Cartoon Comrade," published in *Edna*, September, 2010. She lives in Highland, New York with her cat…and….

Colleen Geraghty is a multi-media artist and writer. She is a resident of the Hudson Valley and a member of the Wallkill Valley Writers.

Carol Goodman is the author of eight novels including *The Lake of Dead Languages* and *The Seduction of Water*, which won the 2003 Hammett Prize. Her books have been nominated for the IMPAC award twice and the Simon & Schuster/Mary Higgins Clark Award. *The Seduction of Water,* won the Hammett Prize for Literary Excellence in Crime Writing. Under the pseudonym Juliet Dark, her novel, *The Demon Lover,* was a Booklist top ten Sci Fi/Fantasy book of 2011. Her novels have been translated into thirteen languages. She teaches writing at SUNY New Paltz and lives in the Hudson Valley with her family.

Anne Gorrick is the author of I-Formation (Book 2) (Shearman Books, 2012), I-Formation (Book 1) (Shearsman, 2010), and Kyotologic (Shearman, 2008). She collaborated with artist Cynthia Winika to produce a limited edition artists' book, "Swans, the ice". She curates the reading series, Cadmium Text www.cadmiumtextseries.blogspot.com and co-curates, with Lynn Behrendt the electronic journal Peep/Show at www.peepshowpoetry.blogspot.com. Her visual work can be seen at: www.theropedanceraccompaniesherself.blogspot.com. She lives in West Park, New York.

Lee Gould's poems, reviews and essays have appeared in *Quarterly West, the Gay and Lesbian Review, The Berkshire Review. Bridges, Chronogram, Magma, Phoebe, the Literary Gazette, Passager, Women and the Environment* and other journals in the United States, Canada and England. Her chapbook, *Weeds,* was published by Finishing Line Press in 2010. After teaching at Goucher College in Maryland, she retired to the Hudson Valley where she teaches poetry, guide workshops and writes.

Roberta Gould as published widely. Individual poems have appeared in the *Green Mountain Review, Confrontations, New York Times, Chronogram, Borderlands,* in 5 anthologies and in 8 books, including *Writing Air Written Water, EstaNaranja. Not By Blood Alone , Only Rock, Louder Than Seeds.* Her new manuscript is entitled: *Invisible Mountain* .She currently studies entomology and lives near Ashokan Reservoir. Web site, blog: www.robertagould.net or http://robertagould.wordpress.com

Lea Graham is the author of *Hough & Helix & Where & Here & You, You, You* (No Tell Books 2011) and the chapbook, *Calendar Girls* (above ground press, 2006) and has published in journals and anthologies including *American Letters & Commentary, The City Visible, Notre Dame Review,* and the *Capilano Review.* Her translations are forthcoming in *The Alteration of Silence: Recent Chilean Poetry* through the University of New Orleans Press. She is Assistant Professor of English at Marist College in Poughkeepsie, New York, and a native of Northwest Arkansas.

Sari Grandstaff's work has been published in many journals and anthologies including *Chronogram, Pirene's Fountain, Rose & Thorn, Modern Haiku, Riverine: An Anthology of Hudson Valley Writers* (Codhill Press), *Contemporary Haibun, volume 12* (Red Moon Press) *and Lifeblood: Woodstock Poetry Society Anthology* (Chickaree Press). She is a high school librarian and a member of the Hudson Valley Haiku-kai and the Haiku Society of America.

Carol Graser runs the poetry reading series at Saratoga's legendary Caffè Lena and has performed her work at various events and venues around New York. Her work's been published in many literary journals, and she is the author of the poetry collection, *The Wild Twist of Their Stems* (Foothills Publishing).

Morgan Gwenwald is a Hudson Valley writer and photographer. Her photo of the Hudson River was chosen to be the cover image for a previous Codhill Press anthology, *WaterWrites: A Hudson River Anthology.* She is on staff at the Sojourner Truth Library on the campus of SUNY New Paltz.

Josepha Gutelius writes plays, short stories, and poetry. A Pushcart Prize nominee, Eric Hoffer Award finalist, and a story chosen for *Best New Writing 2013*. Her poetry and prose have appeared in *Juked, Rain Taxi, BlazeVOX, Offcourse, Blue Lake Review, Salt River, Backhand Stories, Sein und Werden*, Argotist, *Triggerfish Critical Review, Jivin' Ladybug, EWR: Short Stories*, among others. Full-length plays, *Veronica Cory* and *Miracle Mile,* are published in stageplays.com and Professional Playscripts Publishers. Her companion plays, *RASP/Elektra* were featured in *The Modern Review* (and forthcoming from Muse Cafe Press). Website: josephagutelius.com

Janet Hamill is the author of five volumes of poetry. Her most recent, *Body of Water* (Bowery Books), was nominated for the Poetry Society of America's William Carlos Williams prize. Her poems, "K-E-R-O-U-A-C" and "The Wanderer," were both nominated for the Pushcart Prize. A strong advocate of the spoken word, she has released two CD's in collaboration with the bands Moving Star and Lost Ceilings. She presently serves on the artists' advisory board at the Seligmann Center for the Arts in Sugar Loaf.

Ruth D. Handel's poems have appeared in anthologies and literary journals including *Common Ground Review, Westchester Review, The Jewish Women's Literary Annual, Clockwise Cat, Contemporary Haibun Online,* and *Evening Street Review.* She has published a chapbook, *Reading the White Spaces* (Finishing Line Press, 2009), and completed a second manuscript. She teaches workshops in poetry writing and manages the Poetry Caravan, a volunteer organization of 30 Westchester poets who bring poetry to the community.

Pamela Hart is writer-in-residence at the Katonah Museum of Art, Katonah, New York, where she directs a visual literacy education program. She was a poetry writing fellow in 2011 at the SUNY Purchase College Writers Center. Her poetry has been published in print and online journals, including *Kalliope, Lumina, Rattapalax, The Cortland Review, qarrtsiluni* and others. She is a curator for Lift Trucks Projects, an arts space in Croton Falls, New York. Her chapbook, *The End of the Body*, was published by Toadlily Press in 2006. For the last two years she has been a writing mentor at the Afghan Women's Writing Project. She was awarded a 2013 Poetry Fellowship from the National Endowment for the Arts.

Sandra Sturtz Hauss's poetic essays have appeared on greeting cards, in calendars, and in anthologies published by Blue Mountain Arts. Her poems have been published online and in paperback journals. A retired teacher of gifted/talented students, she belongs to the Westchester Poetry Caravan and is currently working on a chapbook.

Adrienne Hernandez's poems have appeared in or have been accepted for publication in *The Mid-America Poetry Review, Big City Lit, The Westchester Review, The Teacher's Voice, Cyclamens and Swords, Lilliput Review, Wisconsin Review* and other journals. She has facilitated inter-generational poetry writing workshops and has been a featured poet at the Cornelia Street Café, the Hudson Valley Writer's Center, and the Ridgefield Theater Barn.

Claire Hero is the author of *Sing, Mongrel* and three chapbooks: *Dollyland, afterpastures*, and *Cabinet*. Her poems and stories have appeared in *A Public Space, Black Warrior Review, Columbia Poetry Review, Denver Quarterly,* and elsewhere. She has lived in the Hudson Valley since 2008.

Heather Hewett has published essays in a range of publications, including *The Washington Post*; CNN.com; *The Women's Review of Books*; *Brain, Child: The Magazine for Thinking Mothers*; *Kaleidoscope*; and *Ducts*. She also blogs for Girl with Pen (www.girlwpen.com). She is an associate professor of

English and Women's, Gender, and Sexuality Studies at the State University of New York at New Paltz. Born and bred in Oklahoma, she lives in the lower Hudson Valley with her family.

Mala Hoffman is a freelance writer and educator who lives in Gardiner, New York. Her work has appeared in the *Village Voice, Chronogram, Awosting Alchemy, Edna,* and *Riverine,* among others. Her chapbook, *Half Moon over Midnight,* was published by Paper Kite Press in 2006.

Maryann Hotvedt is the author of the short story, "The Corner Store," which won the Santa Cruz Libraries Prose Award in 2002. These days she is working on her first collection of poems, *Chain Lightning.* Poems from the collection have been published in the Hudson Valley publication, Chronogram.

Kate Hymes is a poet and educator living in New Paltz, New York. She has been a featured reader at many local venues. Her poems have been published in journals and anthologies, most recently the Cave Canem 10 Year Anniversary Anthology, *Gathering Ground* (University of Michigan Press). Kate leads writing workshops in New Paltz and co-leads the workshop, "If We Are Sisters: Black and White Women Write Across Race," with Pat Schneider, Director Emeritus of Amherst Writers and Artists. www.wallkillvalleywriters.com

Rachel Z. Ikins has won ten poetry prizes, among them First Place, National League of American Penwomen, 2006 and 2008. Her chapbooks include *Slide-show in the Woods* (Foothills 2008), *Transplanted* (Finishing Line Press 2010) and *Renovation* (Foothills 2012). She is a member of the Penwomen CNY Chapter and a long distance member of Every Other Thursday Night Poetry Group in Vorheesville, NY.

Susan Jefts lives in Saratoga Springs, New York and works as a mentor at Empire State College. Many of her poems have been inspired by her explorations of such mountainous regions as the Adirondacks, Vermont, and Scotland, and can be found in *Blue Stone Review, Parnassus Literary Journal, the Literary Gazette,* and various other journals and anthologies. She has a chapbook, *Bended Moments,* and is working on her first full-length book of poetry.

Bobbi Katz grew up in Newburgh during radio days. She fell in love with jazz as a young child, dancing and making up rhymes to the music. When her own children were teens, she worked as an editor for Random House for a dozen years and has published over eighty books for kids and educators, including collections of her own poems and half a dozen anthologies. Her poems and essays for grown-ups have been published in various anthologies. Her current project is a memoir, Ain't Misbehavin'. www.bobbikatz.com

Judith Kerman has published seven collections of poetry, most recently *Galvanic Response* (March Street Press), and two books of translations of Cuban and Dominican women poets (White Pine Press, BOA Editions). She was a Fulbright Scholar in the Dominican Republic in 2002. She runs Mayapple Press, located in Woodstock, New York.

Christine Boyka Kluge is the author of *Stirring the Mirror* and *Teaching Bones to Fly*, both from Bitter Oleander Press. Her chapbook, *Domestic Weather*, won the Uccelli Press Chapbook Contest. Her work has appeared in many anthologies and magazines. She is also an artist and lives in Rhienbeck, New York.

Alison Koffler received the Poetry Teacher of the Year award in 2003, the Bronx Council on the Arts' BRIO Award for poetry in 1993, 2000 and 2006, and she won the 2011 Green Heron Poetry Contest. Her poems appear in numerous publications and she works for the New York City Writing Project at Lehman College.

Kateri Kosek's poetry has appeared in journals such as *Orion, South Dakota Review, Crab Orchard Review, Third Coast,* and *Rhino,* and her essays in *Creative Nonfiction, Blueline,* and *Terrain.org.* She grew up in the Hudson Valley, graduated from Vassar College, and holds an M.F.A. from Western Connecticut University.

Raphael Kosek is a life-long Hudson Valley resident whose poetry has appeared in *Commonweal,*

New Millennium, Water-Stone, and the Frost Foundation website. Her chapbook, *Letting Go,* was published by Finishing Line Press (2009). Her poetry has received two Dutchess County Arts Council fellowships. "Seascape 2" won first prize from the Lawrence Durrell Society and just appeared in their journal, *Deus Loci.*

Leslie LaChance's work has appeared in various journals and anthologies, including *Quiddity, OVS, Juked, The Greensboro Review, Birmingham Poetry Review, JMWW, Chronogram* and *Apple Valley Review.* She has been nominated for a Pushcart Prize and has received a Best of the Net award from *Sundress.* Born and raised in the Hudson Valley, Leslie currently lives in Nashville, Tennessee, where she edits *Mixitini Matrix: A Journal of Creative Collaboration* and teaches at a small university nearby.

Ann Lauinger's book, *Persuasions of Fall* (University of Utah Press, 2004), won the Agha Shahid Ali Prize in Poetry. Recent and forthcoming poems appear in *Common Ground Review, Global City Review, Lumina, The Same,* and *The Southern Poetry Review.* She is a member of the SlaperingHol Press Advisory Committee and lives in Ossining, NY.

Sharmagne Leland-St. John is a Native American poet, concert performer, lyricist, artist, and filmmaker. Her work can be found in a multitude of anthologies and on-line literary journals. She has published 4 collection of poetry: *Unsung Songs, Silver Tears and Time, Contingencies,* and *La Kalima,* and has co-authored a book on film production design. *Designing Movies: Portrait of a Hollywood Artist* (Greenwood/Praeger, 2006).

Nadine May Lewis has been an artist-in-residence through The Artist Habitat at the Kingston Library. Her work was selected for a book cover through Atropos Press, Dresden. She has written several chapbooks including *Damning the Muse!* And *Between Belly and Womb* and edited *Core Pieces and Literary Passions,* among others. She has a sketchbook with the Brooklyn Art Library. She is married to Reverend Dr. Gregory Bray and is the proud mother of Eamon and Nora.

Lyn Lifshin has published over 130 books including 3 from Black Sparrow. Recent books: *Ballroom, All the Poets (Mostly) Who Have Touched me, Living and Dead. All True, Especially the Lies, Knife Edge* & *Absinthe: The Tango Poems,* and *For the Roses poems after Joni Mitchell.* www.lynlifshin.com

Priscilla Lignori completed a seven-year course of study in writing and teaching haiku with haiku master Clark Strand, author of *Seeds From a Birch Tree.* She's been published in *Ko, Asahi Haikuist, Mainichi Daily News, World Haiku Review,* and elsewhere. Ms. Lignori funded Hudson Valley Haiku-kai, a monthly haiku group in Woodstock, New York.

Iris Litt is the author of two books of poems and has had poems and short stories published in many magazines, including *Confrontation, Onthebus, Pearl, Asphodel, Earth's Daughters, Traveler Tales, Pacific Coast Journal.* She has led writing workshops in Woodstock since 1995.

Mary Makofske's book *Traction* (Ashland Poetry Press, 2011) won the Richard Snyder Award. Her poems have appeared in *Poetry, Mississippi Review, Natural Bridge, Poetry East, Louisville Review, Asheville Poetry Review,* and other journals and several anthologies. She is also the author of *The Disappearance of Gargoyles* and *Eating Nasturtiums,* winner of a Flume Press Chapbook Award. She won the 2012 Poetry Prize from *The Ledge.*

Claire McGuire is a poet and student working towards a Master's degree in World Heritage Studies. Her work has been featured in several local and regional publications and online literary collections. She is currently exploring the world outside of the Hudson Valley, and is for the moment living and writing in eastern Germany.

Linda Melick lives in New Paltz, New York. She has had two poems recently published online in *Obsession Literary Magazine* and a memoir piece in *Tiny Lights Journal.* She was the recipient of a National Endowment for the Humanities grant to study African poetry.

Marion Menna has had poems published in *West Hills Review '84, Long Island Quarterly, Xanadu, Stone Canoe II, Waterwrites, Avocet,* and *Hurricane Blues, MSU 2005.* Her chapbooks include: *An Unknown Country* (Finishing Line Press 2009) and *Deep Ecology* (Benevolent Bird Press, 2011). A short story, "An Enormous Child" is online at Persimmon Tree (Spring 2009).

Karen Michel lives in slightly upstate New York in a house made from a log cabin kit. Formerly, she lived in log cabins-real ones-in Alaska, without running water or indoor toilets. Michel, who regularly contributes to NPR's "All Things Considered" and "Morning Edition" as a cultural correspondent, is an educator and a multi-media artist incorporating sound, text, visuals and performance.

Tana Miller is a fifty-year resident of the Hudson Valley, with a lingering southern sensibility, due to being born in Birmingham, Alabama. "I am shaped by words—by their sound, their shape, their meaning—and consider poetry my way to say, 'Here I am.'"

Georganna Millman lives in the Catskill Mountains. Her poems have appeared in *Hunger Mountain, The Margie Review, Blueline, Home Planet News, Chronogram,* and others. She has published two chapbooks of poetry, *Formulary* and *Set Theory.* She is enrolled in the M.F.A. program at Vermont College of Fine Arts.

Mimi Moriarty is the poetry editor for *The Spotlight,* a local weekly newspaper in the Hudson Valley. She has two chapbooks published by Finishing Line Press: *War Psalm,* which came out in 2007, and *Sibling Reverie,* co-authored with her brother, Frank Desiderio, published in the spring of 2012. A third chapbook, *Crows Calling,* will be published by Foothills Press in 2013.

Karen Neuberg lives in Brooklyn and West Hurley, New York. Her poems have appeared in numerous publications including the anthologies, *Riverine* and *Child of My Child.* Her chapbook, *Detailed Still,* was published by Poets West Prada Press. She is the editor of *Inertia Magazine* and associate editor of *First Literary Review-East.*

Irene O'Garden's writing has found its way to the Off-Broadway stage (*Women On Fire*, Samuel French), and into hardcover (*Fat Girl,* Harper). Her children's book, *Forest What Would You Like?* is published by Holiday House and her Pushcart Prize-Winning essay, "Glad To Be Human," was published in e-book form from Untreed Reads. She's received fellowships, residencies and awards for her writing. *www.ireneogarden.com*

Jo Pitkin is the author of *The Measure* (Finishing Line Press) and the forthcoming *Commonplace Invasions* (Salmon Poetry). Her award-winning poems are published in *Little Star, Nimrod, Quarterly West, Ironwood, Stone Canoe, BigCityLit, Riverine,* and other journals and anthologies. She lives near the narrowest and deepest part of the Hudson River.

Deborah Poe is the author of the poetry collections *Our Parenthetical Ontology* (2008), *Elements* (2010), and *the last will be stone,* too (2013), novella in verse, *Hélène* (2012) and several chapbooks, most recently *Keep* (above/ground press). She co-edited *Between Worlds: An Anthology of Contemporary Fiction and Criticism* (Peter Lang) and is currently co-editing *In/Filtration,* a book of Hudson Valley innovative poetics (Station Hill Press). She is assistant professor of English at Pace University. deborahpoe.com

Trina Porte's work appears in the anthologies *lifeblood* and *Just Like a Girl.* She has read at BAAD and Bluestockings in New York, Patrick's Cabaret, and Dyke Night in Minneapolis, and the New Lebanon Library. She's archived at Brooklyn's and Minnesota's Historical Society and lives in the woods with her wife.

Judith Prest is a poet whose work has appeared in *Chronogram, Mad Poets Review, Akros Review, Slightly West, Earth's Daughters* and other journals. Her poetry has been included in the anthologies: *Peer Glass, Layers of Possibility, Beloved on the Earth,* and *Moments of the Soul.*

Gretchen Primack's poems have appeared in *The Paris Review, Prairie Schooner, The Massachusetts Review, FIELD, Antioch Review, Ploughshares,* and other journals. She's the author of a chapbook, *The Slow Creaking of Planets,* (Finishing Line 2007) and a full-length collection, *Kind* (Post-Traumatic Press 2013). An animal activist, she co-wrote *The Lucky Ones: My Passionate Fight for Farm Animals* (Penguin Avery 2012) with Jenny Brown. www.gretchenprimack.com.

Carolyn Quimby is a fourth-year creative writing major at SUNY New Paltz. She's an aspiring memoir writer who's previously been published in *Stonesthrow Review*. She lives on Long Island, but her heart lies in the Hudson Valley.

Marilyn Reynolds's life is devoted to writing and painting. Her last solo poetry reading was in conjunction with her painting and drawing exhibition at the Hudson Opera House. Awards have included a residency at the MacDowell Colony, grants from the New York State Council on the Arts, the New York Foundation for the Arts, the Louis Comfort Tiffany, and Pollack-Krasner foundations, among others. Poems are published in Codhill Press anthologies: *Riverine and Waterwrites*.

Cheryl A. Rice's work has appeared in *Baltimore Review, Chronogram, Florida Review, Home Planet News, Mangrove, Metroland, Poughkeepsie Journal, The Temple, Woodstock Times,* and in the anthologies *Wildflowers*, Vol. II (2002: Shivastan Publishing), *Riverine* (2007: Codhill Press) and *For Enid, With Love* (2010: NYQuarterly). She is the author of *Auction* (2004, Flying Monkey Press; 2nd edition 2010), *Girl Poet* (2007, Flying Monkey Productions, CD), *Roses: three poems* (2011, Flying Monkey Press), and *Outside* (2011, Flying Monkey Press). Her poetry blog, *Flying Monkey Productions*, is at http://flyingmonkeyprods.blogspot.com

Anne Richey teaches poetry courses for Bard's Lifetime Learning Institute. Her poems have appeared in both regional and national journals including *Chronogram, Vanguard Voices of the Hudson Valley, WaterWrites,* and *Prima Materia*.

Rachel Elliott Rigolino is an instructor in the English Department at SUNY New Paltz where she teaches Composition. A woman of limited interests, Rachel volunteers at her church, reads a lot (mostly nonfiction), and enjoys going out to the movies.

Karen Rippstein is a poet and creative writing teacher at Westchester Community College, at nature centers, senior centers, and libraries. Karen is recipient of ongoing Poets and Writers, Inc. grants and a member of the Poetry Caravan. Publications include *Journal of Poetry Therapy, Letters from the Heart, Personal Journaling* magazine, *en(compass)*, and *the Poetry Caravan Anthology*.

Abigail Nadell Robin is a writer, teacher, actor, director and producer, now residing in Kingston, New York. She created ART-Abigail Robin Tours, artist studio tours in the Hudson Valley and New York City. She recently co-produced and performed in Howard Zinn's play, *Emma,* about activist Emma Goldman at Woodstock's Byrdcliffe Theatre. Her one-woman show in which she plays Emma Goldman has toured in the Hudson Valley. A memoir, *L'Chaim,* has recently been published.

Susan Fox Rogers is the author of *My Reach: A Hudson River Memoir*, which chronicles her journeys by kayak on the Hudson River. She is the editor of twelve anthologies, including *Solo: On Her Own Adventure,* and *Alaska Passages*. Her anthology, *Antarctica: Life on the Ice,* emerged from a National Science Foundation grant. She teaches the creative essay at Bard College.

Laura Russo has been writing poetry since she was six years old. "Most of my writing has been for my own personal pleasure. I love to write fiction based on personal experience."

Natalie Safir is an editor, lecturer and poetry workshop leader at local colleges and libraries. She developed a Writing as Healing program and has authored five collections of poetry. She is widely published in national journals and anthologies used at the college level. Recently, she taught six sessions on craft at a local library and taught a course in memoir writing at a senior center.

Jo Salas is a New Zealand-born writer of fiction and nonfiction, living in New Paltz. Her short stories have been published in *Prima Materia* and other literary journals. Several have won or been shortlisted for awards. Her nonfiction includes *Improvising Real Life: Personal Story in Playback Theatre,* now published in eight languages.

Judith Saunders is a long-time resident of the Hudson Valley who has published poems, feature articles, humor, and reviews in a variety of periodicals and anthologies. Recent regional credits include *Art Times, Chronogram, Home Planet News, Inkwell, Blueline, Riverine* and *Waterwrites*.

Nationally, her work has appeared in *Poet Lore, Soundings East, The North American Review*, and *The Christian Science Monitor* among others.

Rebecca Schumejda is the author of two full-length collections *Cadillac Men* (New York Quarterly Press, 2012) and *Falling Forward* (sunnyoutside, 2009). She is also the author of chapbooks *From Seed To Sin* (Bottle of Smoke Press, 2011), *The Map of Our Garden* (verve bath, 2009); *Dream Big Work Harder* (sunnyoutside press 2006); *The Tear Duct of the Storm* (Green Bean Press, 2001); and the poem "Logic" on a postcard (sunnyoutside). She received her M.A. in Poetics and Creative Writing from San Francisco State University and her B.A. in English and Creative Writing from SUNY New Paltz. www.rebeccaschumejda.com

Karen Schoemer is the author of Great *Pretenders: My Strange Love Affair with '50s Pop Music* (Free Press, 2006). Her pop-music reviews and criticism have appeared in *Newsweek*, the *New York Times*, *New York* magazine, and many other publications as well as several music anthologies. She lives in Columbia County.

Rhonda Shary is a writer and adjunct professor of English at SUNY New Paltz. Her poems, essays, and short fiction have appeared in several collections and literary journals, including *WaterWrites: A Hudson River Anthology* (2009) and the *Shawangunk Review* (2012).

Laura Jan Shore was raised in the Hudson Valley, was a graduate of Sleepy Hollow High, and raised her children there. Following her grandchildren, she immigrated to Australia in 1996 but returns yearly to visit family. Author of the YA novel, *The Sacred Moon Tree (*Bradbury Press, 1986), she also has published poetry in selected literary magazines in the United States, Italy, New Zealand, and Australia. Her collection, *Breathworks* (Dangerously Poetic Press), was launched at the 2002 Byron Writers Festival. Her latest book, *Water over Stone*, won IP Picks Best Poetry 2011 and is published by Brisbane publisher, Interactive Press.

Micky Shorr facilitates a monthly poetry reading in Kingston, New York. Her poems have been read on WKZE radio, and have been or will be published in *Chronogram, Home Planet News,* the Woodstock Poetry Society anthology, *"Lifeblood"* and the Arts Society of Kingston's chapbook, "25". Micky has been a psychotherapist in NYC and Kingston.

Joan I. Siegel is the author of *Hyacinth for the Soul* (Deerbrook Editions, 2009) and the forthcoming *Light at Point Reyes* (Shabda Press) and co-authored *Peach Girl: Poems for a Chinese Daughter. She is* the recipient of the 1999 *New Letters* Poetry Prize and the 1998 Anna Davidson Rosenberg Award as well as four Pushcart Prize nominations. A recent finalist for *Nimrod*'s 2012 Pablo Neruda Prize, Siegel has published in *The Atlantic Monthly, The American Scholar, The Gettysburg Review Commonweal, Prairie Schooner, Raritan, Carolina Quarterly, Alaska Quarterly Review, North American Review,* among other journals and anthologies. Emerita Professor of English at SUNY/Orange in Middletown, NY, she received SUNY's 2007 Chancellor's Award for Excellence in Teaching.

Donna Spector's play *Golden Ladder* (*Women's Playwrights: The Best Plays of 2002*) was produced Off Broadway, as was her first play, *Another Paradise*. Her poetry volume, *The Woman Who Married Herself*, a Sinclair Poetry Prize finalist, was published by Evening Street Press. Spector won the Masters Poetry Prize; in addition, her poems were nominated three times for the Pushcart Prize.

Jeanne Stauffer-Merle's poetry has appeared in several literary journals including, *The Colorado Review, The Notre Dame Review, The Laurel Review, Sentence, Caketrain*, and the anthology, *The Cento* (Red Hen). She is the author of one poetry chapbook, *Here in the Ice House* (Finishing Line). A second chapbook is forthcoming by Plumberries Press.

Margo Taft Stever's chapbook, *The Hudson Line* (Main Street Rag, 2012), was an editor's choice; *Frozen Spring* (2002) was the winner of the Mid-List Press First Series Award for Poetry; and *Reading the Night Sky* won the 1996 Riverstone Poetry Chapbook Competition. She is the founder of The Hudson Valley Writers' Center and founding editor of SlaperingHol Press.

Victoria Sullivan, poet and a playwright, has had seven Equity productions in New York City.

Currently active in the Woodstock Fringe Playwrights Unit, she has performed her poetry throughout the Hudson Valley, has three published chapbooks, and is the "poet laureate of the Woodstock Roundtable" on WDST 100.1.

Teresa Sutton is a teacher and a poet, who earned an M.F.A. in poetry from Pine Manor College. Her first poetry book, *They're Gone*, was published by Finishing Line Press in 2012. Her poems have appeared in *Fourteen Hills, Solstice: A Magazine of Diverse Voices, Memoir (and), Peregrine: Amherst Writers, California Quarterly, The Healing Muse*, and many others. She lives in Poughkeepsie, New York, and is the mother of two children.

Eva Tenuto studied acting at American Academy of Dramatic Arts and went on to found The Women's Experimental Theater Group which performed at various venues in New York City and East Coast colleges for over a decade. She most recently developed TMI Project, a memoir writing workshop in which real-life stories are shaped into well-crafted monologues and performed by the people who lived them. She is honored to be a part of the transformation of so many people's stories.

Meredith Trede's new book of poems, *Field Theory*, was published by Stephen F. Austin State University Press in October 2011. She is a founding publisher of Toadlily Press. Her chapbook, *Out of the Book*, was in *Desire Path*, the inaugural volume of The Quartet Series and has been published in *Barrow Street, Blue Mesa Review, Gargoyle,* and *The Paris Review*. She has been awarded residency fellowships at Blue Mountain Center, Ragdale, Saltonstall, the Virginia Center for the Creative Arts in Virginia and France, and the 2012 Nicholson Political Poetry Award. She was awarded the James J. Nicholson Political Poetry Prize in April 2012.

Lorna Tychostup has over fifteen years' experience as an international journalist, photographer, and communications consultant, began her writing career scrawling poems on napkins and covering town and school board meetings for mid-Hudson Valley publications. As Senior Editor of *Chronogram Magazine,* her reporting took her to Mexico, Morocco, and the Middle East, with a long-term focus on Iraq. She has a B.A. in Cultural Studies from Empire State College, SUNY New Paltz and an M.S. from New York University's Center for Global Affairs.

Pauline Uchmanowicz's poems, essays, and reviews have appeared in *Crazyhorse, Indiana Review, Ohio Review, Massachusetts Review, New American Writing, Ploughshares, Provincetown Arts Journal, Radcliffe Quarterly, Southern Poetry Review, West Branch, Woodstock Times*, and *Z Magazine*. She is an associate professor of English at the State University of New York at New Paltz.

Barbara Louise Unger's latest book, *Charlotte Bronte, You Ruined My Life* (The Word Works 2011) was a poetry best-seller for SPD. Her second book, *The Origin of the Milky Way*, won the Gival Press Poetry Award among others. She is an English professor at the College of Saint Rose in Albany.

Kappa Waugh is the daughter, grandchild and wife of poets. Suffering poetry abuse from an early age, she decided if you can't fight 'em, join 'em. She has published in *Proof Rock* and *Legacies*. She lives in Port Ewen, New York, and glories in her view of the Roundout.

Ethel Wesdorp is a 2001 graduate of SUNY New Paltz, and works there in the English Department. She enjoys spending time with her family and friends, listening to bluegrass and folk music, quilting and knitting, reading and writing, and playing *Scrabble* and *Words With Friends*. She has published poems in *WaterWrites* and *From Penn's Store to The World*.

Nancy Willard was educated at the University of Michigan and Stanford University. She has written two novels, seven books of stories and essays, and twelve books of poetry. A winner of the Devins Memorial Award, she has had NEA grants in both fiction and poetry. Her book *Water Walker* was nominated for the National Book Critics Circle Award. She won the Newbery Medal for *A Visit to William Blake's Inn*. Her most recent book of poems is *The Sea at Truro*.

Amelia B. Winkler is a poet, writer and teacher. Her essays and articles have been published in *The New York Times, The Jewish Week, North County News* and *Women's News*. Her poems have appeared in *Big City Lit, Jewish Currents, Red Owl, The Westchester Review* and other small presses and anthologies. A former high school English teacher in Buffalo, New York and Needham, Massachusetts, she teaches in writing programs co-sponsored by Poets & Writers and the Arts and Culture Council of Greenburgh, New York.

Caroline Wolfe is the pen name of Marcia Roth Tucci who writes environmental poetry and published in *WaterWrites: A Hudson River Anthology*. She wrote essays for an on-line, women's journal, Moondance.org and published in *Henry: a Hudson Valley Journal*. She currently works in advising and composition at SUNY New Paltz.

Michelle Woods teaches in the English Department at SUNY New Paltz. She is the author of *Translating Milan Kundera* (2006) and *Censoring Translation: Censorship, Theatre and the Politics of Translation* (2012). She lives in Cold Spring, New York.

Sarah Wyman writes along the edges of her Hudson River Valley garden. She has schooled and been schooled in Roanoke, Virginia, Chapel Hill, North Carolina, and at the University of Konstanz in southern Germany. Sarah now teaches literature at the State University of New York at New Paltz.

CREDITS

The following works have originally appeared in the following journals or volumes:

Edie Abrams. "Edie's Mikveh." Published in *Mermaid in Metamorphosis*, Benedict Bird Press, Rootdrinker Institute, 2011.

Sally Bliumis-Dunn. "In the Women's Locker Room." Published in *Walking Under Water*, Wind Publications, 2007.

Lisa Fleck Dondiego. "An Explanation to My Husband: for Christa McAuliffe." Published in *A Sea Change,* Finishing Line Press, 2011.

Lea Graham. "Crushed in Poughkeepsie Time." Published in *Notre Dame Review* (2010). It was also included in her volume, *"Hough & Helix & Where & Here & You, You, You.* No Tell Books, 2011.

Josepha Gutelius. "Valentine." Published in *Salt River Review.*

Adrienne Hernandez. "Duck Pond in Tuckahoe." Published in *The Westchester Review.*

Claire Hero. "reviving Coyote." Published in *Dollyland.* Tarpaulin Sky Press, 2012.

Heather Hewett. *The Valley of the Kings.* Originally published as "A restorative lunch for cyclists in Loire" in *The Philadelphia Inquirer,* September 29, 2002.

Maryann Hotvedt. "Nothing Is Cool." *Chronogram* (February 2010).

Bobbi Katz. "When Granny Made My Lunch." Published in *A Break in the Blue*, Harper Collins, 2001.

Raphael Kosek. "A Wife for the Twenty-First Century." Published in *Letting Go,* Finishing Line Press, 2009.

Ann Lauinger. "Portrait of a Woman with Windex." Published in *Cincinnati Review.*

Priscilla Lignori. Three Haiku. *World Haiku Review,* August 2010, Honorable Mention; 15th Mainichi Haiku Contest 2011, Honorable Mention; *The Mainichi Daily News,* Jan. 6, 2011.

Mary Makofske. "My Father, 1928." Published in *Calyx: A Journal of Art and Literature by Women*, Vol 24, #3 (Summer 2008).

Karen Neuberg. "Try Attaching Sensation to the Figure in Memory." Published in *Sliver of Stone.*

Irene O'Garden. "What You Will Believe." Published in *The Arms of Words: Poems for Disaster Relief,* Sherman Asher Publishing, 2006.

Judith Saunders. "Housewife Sheds Her Skin Like a Snake." Published in *The Panhandler Chapbook Series.*

Laura Jan Shore. "Navigating with Mother." Published in *Water Over Stone*, Interactive Press, Brisbane, Australia.

Joan I. Siegel. "Penelope." Published in *West Branch #66*, (Spring/Summer 2010) and also in *Light at Point Reyes*, Shabda Press, 2012.

Jeanne Stauffer-Merle. "And the Sky Opens." Published in *Here in the Ice House,* Finishing Line Press, 2013.

Margo Taft Stever. "Wind Innuendo." Published in *Rattapallax* and her chapbook, *The Hudson Line*, Main Street Rag, 2012.

Lorna Tychostup. "To the Unnamed One." Published in *Tales from the Revolution.* http://alvapressinc

Meredith Trede. "Between Now and Never." Published in *Field Theory.*

Nancy Willard. "Ilse's Sleep." Published in *Water Walker,* Alfred A. Knopf, 1989.

Amanda B. Winkler. "Waking at Night" (an excerpt). Published in *Waking at Night*, Finishing Line Press, 2013.

Sarah Wyman. "Wet Exit." Published in *Pertrichor Review 3* (2013).